jim thompson
wild town

James Meyers Thompson was born in Anadarko,
Oklahoma, in 1906. He began writing fiction at a very
young age, selling his first story to *True Detective*
when he was only fourteen. In all, Jim Thompson
wrote twenty-nine novels and two screenplays (for
the Stanley Kubrick films *The Killing* and *Paths
of Glory*). Films based on his novels include: *Coup
de Torchon (Pop. 1280), Serie Noire (A Hell of a
Woman), The Getaway, The Killer Inside Me, The
Grifters,* and *After Dark, My Sweet.* A biography
of Jim Thompson will be published by Knopf.

Also by Jim Thompson, available from Vintage Books

After Dark, My Sweet
The Alcoholics
The Criminal
The Getaway
The Grifters
A Hell of a Woman
The Killer Inside Me
Nothing More Than Murder
Pop. 1280
Recoil
Savage Night
A Swell-Looking Babe

wild town

wild town

jim thompson

VINTAGE CRIME / **BLACK LIZARD**

vintage books • a division of random house, inc. • new york

First Vintage Crime/Black Lizard Edition, January 1993

Library of Congress Cataloging-in-Publication Data
Thompson, Jim, 1906–1977.
Wild town/by Jim Thompson. — 1st Vintage Crime/Black Lizard ed.
p.   cm. — (Vintage Crime/Black Lizard)
ISBN 0-679-73312-4 (pbk.)
I. Title.   II. Series.
PS3539.H6733W5   1993
813′.54 — dc20   92-56367   CIP

Manufactured in the United States of America
10 9 8 7 6 5 4 3 2 1

wild town

Originally, the place had been one of those old-time cattle towns, the kind you see throughout West and Far West Texas. Just another wide place in a dusty road, a sunbaked huddle of false-fronted buildings with sheet-iron awnings extending out to the curb. Then, a guy with a haywire drilling rig had moved in—a wildcatter. And he optioned a lot of leases on his guarantee to drill, and then he predicated the leases for high interest loans. And what with one thing and another—stealing, begging, kiting checks, angling "dry hole" money from the big companies who wanted to see the area tested—he managed to sink a well.

The well blew in for three thousand barrels of high-grade paraffin-base oil a day. Overnight, the town bulged like a woman eight months gone with triplets. A make-do type of woman, say, a to-hell-with-how-I-look type. For the demand for shelter was immediate, and building materials were hard to come by out here in the shortgrass middle of nowhere. Not only that, but it just isn't smart to put much money into boom-town property. Booms have a way of fizzling out. A lake of oil can go dry the same as any other kind of lake.

So practically all the new structures were temporary—built as cheaply as possible and as quickly as possible. Shacks of wallboard and two-by-fours. Rough-planked, unfinished and unpainted sheds. Houses—and these predominated in the makeshift jungle—that were half frame and half canvas. Tent-houses they were called, or more commonly, rag-houses. And gnawed at by sulphur and salt-spray, they had the look of rags. They stretched out across the prairie in every direction, squatting and winding through the forest of derricks. Shabby, dingy, creaking with the ever-present wind, senile while still in their nonage: a city of rags, spouting—paradoxically?—on the very crest of great riches.

That was the general order of things. The outstanding exception to it was the fourteen-story Hanlon Hotel, built, named after, and owned in fee simple by the wildcatter who had brought in the discovery well. Most people regarded it as proof that all wildcatters are crazy, their insanity increasing in proportion to their success. They pointed to the fact that Hanlon had been blasted out of his drilling rig by the first wild gush of oil, and that the subsequent sixty-foot fall had doubtless been as injurious to his brain as it was to his body.

They may have been right, at that; Mike Hanlon guessed that they might be, sometimes, when his head got to hurting. But just as he'd always been a hell-for-leather guy, not giving a good goddamn for what, he didn't give one now. His wildcatting days were over. Death had claimed his legs, and it was creeping slowly but implacably upward. Still, he'd wanted to stay near the oil, *his* oil, the oil that all the damned fools had said wasn't there. And he wanted to live right for a change, in something besides a crummy flea-bag or cot-house.

So he built the hotel—simply because he wanted to, and because his money was certain to outlast his ability to want. For the same reason he acquired a good-looking wife, marrying a gal who applied for a hostess job. That she was something less than virginal he was sure. Male or female, none but the sinners sought jobs in a ragtown hotel. And Joyce—to give her name—had probably wiggled further on her back than he had traveled on foot.

But what of it, anyway? shrugged Mike Hanlon. He himself had slept with practically everything that couldn't outrun him. Such activities were denied him now, by virtue of his accident, but he saw not a reason in the world why she should share his deprivation. Just so long as she was decent about it—careful—it was okay with him. Just so long as she didn't cause talk, make him look like a damned fool.

That was all he asked or expected of her. That and, of course, looking pretty, and being nice to him. Chewing the fat with him, you know. Cracking a jug with him when he got the blues. Wheeling him around the hotel, now and then, so that he could see how much the goddamned thieves, his employees, were stealing from him . . . Mike was very much opposed to thieves, and, fortunately for them, he'd caught none redhanded yet. Having been a clever thief himself, he knew the very serious danger they represented to men of property.

But getting back to Joyce. He expected little of her, and asked less; not even that she should occupy the same suite that he did. And on a not-too-distant someday, she would inherit everything he owned. So he was sure that their arrangement would work out fine. Why wouldn't it? he asked himself. Why shouldn't she be satisfied?

There was no reason that he could think of. She was riding a good horse, and she should have been content to stick with it for the distance. But, gradually, he became aware that she wasn't. Not that she was guilty of any overt acts. There was nothing he could put his finger on. Still, he knew; he had a hunch about her. And with good reason, he trusted his hunches.

He tried easing up on his already few demands. That wasn't the answer. He became more demanding, clamping down hard in the dough department. Instinct—his hunch—told him that he still wasn't scoring. He couldn't get at it, somehow, the impatience or sheer orneriness or whatever it was that was prodding her toward murder. And, no, he simply couldn't kick her out. Or, rather, he couldn't do it without giving her a fifty-fifty split of his wealth. Their marriage contract so stipulated, and the contract couldn't be broken.

If he divorced her—fifty-fifty. If she divorced him, or "otherwise separated herself from his place of domicile," she was to receive nothing, "the dollar and other valuable considerations already paid over to be considered a full and equal half of the said Mike Hanlon's estate."

Well, of course, Mike wasn't even about to buy his way off of the spot. He'd never done it before, and he sure as hell wasn't going to begin at his age. Anyway—anyway, he thought bitterly—she probably wouldn't go for half split. She struck him as a whole-hog player, that little lady. If he offered her less, gave her reason to believe that she was going to get less, she might drop the drill on him immediately. So he rocked along, worrying and wondering. Getting as jumpy as a bit on granite.

Finally, he made a hypothetical exposure of his problem to the chief deputy sheriff, who, practically speaking, *was* the sheriff and all law in the county as well. The interview was something less than reassuring.

The chief was West Texas "old family," a guy named Lou Ford. For a man who was almost perpetually smiling, he was undoubtedly the most aggravating, disconcerting son-of-a-bitch of all the sons-of-bitches Hanlon had known.

"Well, let's see now," he drawled. "You say this fellow's wife is out to get him. But she's never done nothing against him so far, and he's got no proof that she plans to. So the question is, what can he do about it. I got the straight of it, Mr. Hanlon?"

"That's right."

Ford frowned, shrugged, and shook his head with smiling helplessness. "Let me ask you one, Mr. Hanlon. If a bitch wolf can couple with a dog and a half in a day and a half, how long does it take her to come in heat on a rainy morning?"

"Huh? *Wh-aat?*" Hanlon roared. "Why, you goddamned snooty bastard! I—Wait! Come back here!"

"Just as soon as I borry a gun," Ford promised, on his way to the door. "Don't never carry one myself."

"A gun? But—but—"

"Or maybe you'd like to take back that 'bastard'? Sure wish you would. Don't seem quite right somehow shootin' a fella in a wheelchair."

There was a wistful note in his voice, sudden death in his eyes. He looked at Hanlon, smiling his gentle smile, and an icy chill ran up the wildcatter's spine. Grudgingly he made an apology, tacking on an insult at its end.

"Should have known you wouldn't do anything. Too damned busy taking graft."

"Aw, Mis-ter Hanlon." The chief deputy appeared shocked. "You mean you don't think I'm honest, Mis-ter Hanlon?"

"Think, hell! I *know!* You're the bag-man for that whole stinking courthouse crowd. Wouldn't surprise me a damned bit if you and her were in this deal together."

"Aw, heck. Gosh all fish-hooks. Gee willikers," drawled Ford. "And here we-all thought we had you fooled!"

"You won't get away with it, by God! I'll show you! I'll call in the Texas Rangers!"

"About what, Mis-ter Hanlon? What are you goin' to tell 'em?"

"Well—well, dammit, I told you! I—"

"Didn't hear nothing but a riddle myself. Didn't hear no complaint, or nothing to make a complaint out of."

"So all right, dammit! I can't make one. She hasn't actually done anything to complain about. But—but there must be something . . ." He scowled at the deputy, his voice trailing away helplessly.

Ford shook his head in a grotesque mockery of sadness. "Now, it sure seems like there ought to be somethin' to do, don't it?" he said. "Yes, sir, it sure does, and that's a fact. Too bad I'm so dadblamed dumb."

"Get out!" said Hanlon hoarsely.

"You sure you want me to? You wouldn't just like to laze around and swap riddles?"

"I said to get out!"

"Well, maybe I better," Lou Ford nodded agreeably. "Got a gambling house I ain't shook down yet today."

He left, rocking in his high-heeled boots. Hanlon guessed that he'd really made a mess of things. That Ford was a grafter, he was positive. But it had been stupid to say so. These West Texans were a breed apart, prideful, easily offended, steadfast friends and the bitterest of enemies. They were at once blunt and delicate of speech. They had their own code of ethics, their own standards of what was right and wrong. Unbendingly intolerant of some transgressions, they blandly overlooked others that were nominally worse.

Only recently, for example, a man had received a two-year prison sentence for beating a horse. In the same week, a case of burglary was dismissed against a man who had broken into a liquor store. He was broke, you see, and he had a Godawful hangover—that which, as everyone knew, there is nothing worse. So he had broken into the store to get a drink, because he really needed a drink, you know. And maybe it was kind of the wrong thing to do—kind of against the law, maybe—but a fella that really needs a drink ain't rightly responsible for what he does . . .

Yea, Hanlon thought drearily. *I really botched things with Ford. I should have been extra-nice to him, asked how he was feeling, asked what he thought about the weather. Complimented him on everything I could think of. Bragged up him and his stinking ancestors clear back to the days of the Spaniards. If I'd done that, if I hadn't hedged with him, if I'd come right out in the open to begin with—*

It wouldn't have made a damned bit of difference, Hanlon decided. Ford had been down on him before the interview; all the regular pre-boom residents of the community were down on him. They'd been swell to him when he first came here—the most likable, open-handed people he'd ever known. But then he'd had to start cutting corners, stretching the truth, making promises that he didn't keep. And, hell, they shouldn't have got sore about it. They should have understood that it was just business, and that every man has to look out for himself in a business deal. But they didn't understand. They didn't, and they would have no part of apologies or explanations. As far as they were concerned, he didn't exist. He was just a something that was beneath notice or contempt, the stuck-up, stiff-necked, high-faluting—!

Hanlon snatched up the whiskey decanter and shakily poured himself a huge drink. He threw it down and poured another. And gradually he began to calm. A man can't stay in an uproar all the time. He can worry just so much, and then he has to stop.

A few days later, Joyce ushered a man named McKenna into his suite.

He was somewhere in his late thirties, burly, surly-faced. He had the kind of eyes that always look like they've been crying. He was applying for the job of house detective.

"How about references?" Hanlon asked. "What's your background?"

"What about *your* references?" McKenna said. "What did you do before you latched on to all this?"

Hanlon laughed sourly. "Look kind of pale. Wouldn't have been cooped up somewhere, would you?"

"You want a straight answer, you better ask a straight

question," McKenna said roughly. "Sure, I've been in the pen—five years for killing a boob. And before that I did six months in jail for beating up my wife. And before that I served two years in an Army stockade for taking a shot at a general. And—well, to hell with it, and you too. I'm not making any apologies or asking any favors, so you can take your two-bit job and—"

"Easy," said Hanlon. "Take it easy, McKenna."

It was a trick, of course. No bona fide applicant for a job would be so brutally frank and deliberately unpleasant. Still, the house dick's job was open, and it would have to be filled. And the next applicant . . . what about him? How could one be sure that he was simply after a job and not a life?

And—and here was a hell of a note—Hanlon liked the guy. Yeah, he actually liked this wife-beater and brig-bird, this man who had killed once, and was doubtless all primed to kill again.

"I don't mean to pry, Mr. McKenna," he said politely, "but where is your wife, now?"

"I don't know . . ." Immediately there was a subtle change in McKenna's manner. "I'm no longer married to her—sir."

"Well, that's good. I mean, the house detective lives in here—he's subject to call at all times—and it doesn't work out very well for a married man."

"But"—McKenna looked at him with a mixture of hope and suspicion. "You mean—I get the job?"

"What else? Any reason why you shouldn't get it?" Hanlon said.

And he laughed quietly to himself, at himself, as only a man can laugh when there is nothing else to do.

McKenna's first name was David, but he had been called Bugs for practically as far back as he could remember. It fitted the awkward lummox of a kid who, though only ten years old, was almost as big as his fifth-

grade teacher. It fitted the actions of the frightened child,
the self-doubting, insecure youth, and the introverted,
defensively offensive man. He seemed to have a positive
knack for doing the right thing at the wrong time. For dis-
trusting his friends, and trusting his enemies. For being
ridiculously uncompromising over the trifling, and seemingly indifferent to the nominally vital.

The guy was just nuts, people said, as bugsy as they came.
He couldn't take a joke. He didn't want to be friendly. He'd
climb a tree to make trouble when he could stand on the
ground and have peace. That's what they said about him,
the man he eventually became. And it was reasonably
descriptive of that scowling, sullen, short-tempered man.
Only his eyes belied the description; angrily bewildered
eyes. Eyes that seemed wet with unshed tears, as, perhaps,
they were.

When he finished his five-year prison stretch—and he
served every minute of it, thanks to the outraged and
insulted parole board—Bugs McKenna drifted into Dallas.
He got a job as night dishwasher in a greasy spoon. He
spent most of his daytime hours in the public library. It was
a good way of keeping out of trouble, he thought. Moreover, it didn't cost anything, and there was nothing that he
would rather do.

Well, though, there was a "furtive" look about him, in the
opinion of the librarian. Also, as she pointed out to the
police, he couldn't possibly have any interest in the books
he selected, Kafka, Schopenhauer, Addison and Steele—
now, really, officers!

The cops asked Bugs a few questions. Bugs responded
with a wholly impossible suggestion involving their night-
sticks and a certain part of their anatomy.

Skip the details. Bugs got a rough roust out of Dallas,
leaving town with new knots on his head and fresh bruises
to his spirit.

Walking through the outskirts of Fort Worth, he saw a little girl fall off her tricycle. He picked her up, and dusted her
off. He hunkered down in front of her, joking with her ten-
derly, getting her to smile. And a patrol car drifted into the
curb . . .

Bugs spent two weeks in the Fort Worth jail. At Weatherford, the next town west, he was jugged for three days. In Mineral Wells, he drew another three days of "investigation." He was spitting blood when he emerged from it, but it hadn't softened him a bit. His last words to the cop who escorted him to the city limits were of a type to curl the hair on a brass monkey.

Still, he knew he couldn't take much more; not without a little rest anyway. He had to get the hell away from the cities, the heavily settled areas, and do it fast or he'd damned well be dead. So he left the highways, and took to the freights. He stuck with them, moving inconspicuously from freight to freight, moving steadily westward. And eventually he arrived at the place called Ragtown. That was about as far west as a man could go. As anything but a jack rabbit or a tarantula would have reason for going.

Thirty minutes after his arrival he was in jail.

It was partly his own fault, he admitted reluctantly. Just a little his own fault. Having dropped off the freight, he was in the station rest-room washing up, when a leathery-faced middle-aged man walked in. A silver badge was clipped to his checked shirt. He wore a gunbelt and an ivory-handled forty-five.

As he started to bend over the drinking fountain, Bugs turned from the sink and faced him. He stared at the man, his eyes hard and hateful. Leather-face straightened slowly, a puzzled-polite frown building up on his face.

"Yeah, stranger?" he said. "Something on your mind?"

"What do you mean, what's on *my* mind?" Bugs said. "I'm not stupid. You saw me drop off that freight. You've got me tagged for a bum. So, all right, let's drop the dumb act and get on with the business. I'm David McKenna, alias 'Bugs' McKenna; last permanent address, Texas State Penitentiary; recent addresses, Dallas city jail, Fort Worth city jail, Weatherford city jail, Mineral Wells city—"

"Now, looky"—the man made a baffled gesture. "I mean, what the hell?"

"Come on! Come off of it! I suppose you just followed me in here to get a drink, huh?"

The man started to nod. Then, his squinted gray eyes turned frosty, and his voice dropped to a chilling purr. "Lookin' for trouble, eh?" he said, the words cold-edged but soft. "Just ain't happy without it. Well, I always like to oblige."

The gun whipped up from his hip. Bugs hesitated; nervous, oddly ashamed, wondering why it was that he always had to be in such a hell of a hurry with the mouth.

"Look," he mumbled. "I-I've been catching it pretty rough. I didn't mean to—"

"You look." The hammer of the gun clicked. "Look real good. Now, you want to move or do you want me to move you?"

Bugs moved.

The jail was in the basement of the ancient brick courthouse. The ventilation and the light were bad, but the bunks were clean, and the chow—brought in from one of the town's restaurants—was really first class. Each prisoner got three good meals a day, as opposed to the twice-a-day slop in most jails. He was also given a sack of makings or, if he preferred, a plug of chewing.

Bugs supposed there was a gimmick somewhere in the deal. Probably you'd have pay off with a road gang at twelve hours a day. But such, according to the other prisoners—no local talent, all floaters like himself—was not the case.

"These folks are different out here," an oilfield worker explained. "They throw you in jail, they figure they got to look after you. They might shoot a guy, but they won't starve him to death."

"What about the rough stuff? Working you over until you clean the slate for them?"

"Uh-uh. You ain't done nothin', they won't try to pin it on you. You won't get roughed unless you cut up rough yourself . . . At least," the man added carefully, "they've always played fair with me. This is my fifth time in for drunk and disorderly, and the boys have treated me real nice every time."

"But? There's more to the story?"

"We-el, no, not exactly. Not as far as the treatment of the prisoners is concerned. But the way this town is run"—he shook his head—"I got an idea that there's at least one of these laws, the chief deputy, Lou Ford, that'd just about as soon kill you as look at you. The place is wide open, see? Gambling houses, bootleg joints, honky-tonks. And some very bad babies runnin' 'em. But they don't give any back-talk to Ford. He rides herd on 'em, as easy as I can ride a walking beam."

"He's the chief deputy, you say. What about the sheriff?"

"Sick and old. Hardly ever see him except at election time. So Ford's the man, and I *do* mean the man. He's got the town and the county right in his pocket, and it don't do nothing without his say-so. The funny part about it is, he don't look tough at all: Young, good-looking, always smiling—"

"But a good gunhand, huh?"

"Uh-uh. The only law here that doesn't wear a gun. But, well," the man spread his hands helplessly, "I don't know how he does it; I mean, I couldn't explain. You'd have to see him in action yourself."

Bugs had been jailed early in the morning. The following afternoon, the turnkey took him out of the bullpen and up the stairs to the street floor. He assumed he was being taken into court. Instead, the turnkey handed him a ten-dollar bill and gestured him toward the door.

"That's from Lou Ford," he explained. "Wants to see you, and he figured you might want to spruce up first."

"But—well, what about the charges against me?"

"Ain't any. Lou had 'em dropped. He'll be out to his house when you're ready. Anyone can tell you where it is."

"Now, wait a minute!" Bugs bristled. "What does he want to see me about? What if I don't want to see him?"

"Easy to find out for yourself, mister. If you do see him or if you don't."

Bugs got a shave and a haircut. He bought a white shirt and a tie, and had his worn suit sponged and pressed. Boomtown prices being what they are, that took practically all of the ten. He used the remainder for a shoeshine and a package of cigarettes, and headed for Lou Ford's house.

There were two "old" residential sections. One was the traditional wrong-side-of-the-tracks settlement of the Mexicans and "white trash." The other was up the hill from, and overlooking the town: a few blocks of tree-lined streets, and roomy two-storied houses. Except for color difference—they were usually light blue, white or brown—the houses were almost identical, a comfortable combination of Colonial and Spanish-Moorish architecture. Each had a long porch ("gallery") extending across the front. Despite the area's always uncertain water supply, each had a deep shrub- and tree-shaded lawn.

Ford's house was on the corner. A new Cadillac convertible stood in the driveway. McKenna stepped up on the porch and knocked on the door. There was no answer. He punched the doorbell, discovering that it was out of order. He knocked again. Stooping, he studied the age-dulled brass plate affixed to the door:

Dr. Amos Ford
Enter

The doctor was Lou's father, Bugs had learned. An improvident, kindly man, he had died several years before, leaving nothing to his son but this house, heavily mortgaged at that. Obviously, the sign no longer meant what it said; for visitors to enter, that is. It had been left on the door out of sentiment or shiftlessness. On the other hand . . .

Well, there it was, wasn't it? And why shouldn't a stranger in town take it at its face value? What was he supposed to do—stand out here and beat the skin off his knuckles? He'd been told—*ordered*—to see Ford. Now this sign told him to enter.

Bugs did so.

He was standing in a narrow foyer, quite dark since the doors to the rooms on either side were closed. The only light streamed down from the stairway; from an open door, apparently, right at the head of the stairs. Muted sounds also drifted down the stairs. Scuffling. The creak of bed springs. A man's sardonically soothing drawl, and a woman's quiet, quickly furious voice:

"*Aw, now, Amy. You know I—*"

"*I know you, that's what I know, Lou Ford!*"

"*But she don't mean a thing to me, Amy! Honest. It's just business.*"

"*You're a liar! What kind of business? Well? Go on, I'm listening!*"

"*But I done told you, honey! It's pretty confidential; somethin' I can't talk about. Now, why'n't you just leave it at that, and—*"

There was an outraged sob. The sharp *cra-ack* of a hard-swung palm meeting flesh. Then, the girl came rushing out of the room; weeping in blind anger, clutching a handful of undergarments.

Highlighted by the glare from the door, she began putting on her panties. She got them on, hopping from foot to foot. Then she slumped her shoulders, dropping her breasts into the cups of her brassiere.

That was all that Bugs saw, all that he allowed himself to see. He got quietly back out to the porch, blushing deeply, shamed and embarrassed by what he had seen.

He was like that, oddly. Modest. Excruciatingly old-fashioned, one might say, although he could not regard such things as a matter of fashion. He had killed. He had worked in shabby, disillusioning jobs. He had been penned up with degenerates for years. That had been his environment; violence, foulness and filth. And yet in all his life, he had looked on no more than three naked women. And of the three, one had been his wife.

He wished the third had not been this girl. He wished, with a kind of gnawing hunger, that he had not seen her in her nakedness.

And he wished, longed to see her again: to cherish her, treat her with love and respect. Because, yes, by God, she deserved it! No matter what she'd done, regardless of how things looked.

He'd noticed more than her nakedness—and off-hand he would have said she was not much different than hundreds he'd seen: just a small, well-rounded young woman with a good-featured face and sandy brown hair pulled back in a bun. But than he had gone on looking. And suddenly he had almost gasped at what he saw.

You know how it is. A three-hundred dollar suit doesn't knock your eye out. A Ming vase doesn't shriek for attention. But the ultimate beauty, the perfection, is there; and you'll always see it if you look long enough, see it and recognize it, regardless of whether you've ever seen it before.

Even if you've caught so much crap in your eyes that you're half-blind in one and can't see out of the other . . .

Bugs must have been standing on the porch for ten minutes, kind of dazed and dopey, lost in his own sad thoughts, when he heard the back door close. That snapped him out of it, recalled him to the gray facts of what he was and why he was here. And he knocked again, hastily and loudly.

Ford responded almost immediately with a hail of, "Right with you." A moment later there was the *click-tap* of boots in the hallway, and he opened the door.

"McKenna? I'm Lou Ford. Come on in an' set."

Bugs followed him down the foyer, and into what apparently had been the doctor's one-time office. Ford looked as out of place among the rows of glass-doored bookcases as a man could look.

He was about thirty, the chief deputy. He wore a pinkish-tan shirt, with a black clip-on bowtie, and blue serge pants. The cuffs of the trousers were tucked carelessly into the tops of his boots. In Bugs' book, he stacked up about the same—in appearance—as any county clown.

His black, glossy hair was combed in a straight-back pompadour. His high-arched brows gave his face a droll, impish look. A long thin cigar was clamped between his white even teeth.

He waved Bugs to one of the comfortable leather chairs, then sat himself down behind the desk. He said politely, "Like a drink? Well, how about a cigar, then?" And, then, when Bugs shook his head, "Now, that's right. You're a cigarette smoker, aren't you?"

He said it very carelessly, a man seemingly making conversation. But Bugs was sure that he wasn't. He was saying that he had seen the two cigarette butts which Bugs had flipped onto the sidewalk.

"Just got here, did you?" he went on, subdued amusement in his voice. "Sure hope I didn't keep you waitin'. Nothing I hate worse than a fella that keeps another fella waitin' on him."

"How about crooked cops?" said McKenna. "How do you feel about them?"

"Well . . .which kind you mean? The jailbird kind? The kind that ain't smart enough to stay out of the pen?" Ford grinned at him, narrow-eyed. "Made a little check-back on you, McKenna. You got quite a record."

"There's nothing about grafting in it!"

"Well, now, don't you feel bad about it," Ford said sooth-ingly. "A man can't do everything, and you damned sure done just about everything else."

"Look," Bugs snarled. "What do you—"

"How do you like our fair city, McKenna? Reg'lar little jool of the prairie, ain't it? A city of homes, churches and people. How'd you like to be one with our upstandin', God-fearing citizenry, them homely souls that ain't no more interested in a dollar than I am in my right leg?"

Bugs laughed in spite of himself. He remembered reluc-tantly that, however he might feel about Ford, he was indebted to him.

The deputy joined in his laughter. "Now, that's better," he said. "You got no use for me, maybe. I got none for you, maybe. And maybe we'd both feel different if we could see the other fellow's side. But I reckon that would kind of put us out of step with the world, and it ain't really necessary. We can still do business together."

"What kind of business?"

"There's a big hotel here in town—you saw it, I guess. They need a house dick. Pretty good payin' job, and you get your meals and room along with it. I think I can land it for you."

"Me? I could land a house dick's job in a place like that?"

"You ain't listening." Ford said reprovingly. "I said I could land it for you. Owner's wife is a good friend of mine. Sorry I can't say the same for him."

Bugs hesitated, chewing his lip. His head jerked in a curt negative. "I guess not. I guess I'd better not. I can't get into any more trouble— I *can't*, know what I mean? And if I was sneaked over on some guy, pushed down his throat—"

"You won't be. Won't be no deception, a-tall. Fact is, if I got him figured right, he'll hire you because you have got a sorry record. He ain't been exactly no angel himself, see? And he'll think a guy that comes clean with him must be on the level."

"But I wouldn't be, is that it? That's where you come in."

"Do I?" Ford examined the tip of his cigar. "You know what Confucius say, McKenna? Man with bare ass always have big mouth."

"There's another one I like better," Bugs said. "Many men

drown in their own dung, but few die shouting for a doctor."

"Hey, now!" Ford seemed honestly delighted. "That's all right! But about this hotel job, I ain't askin' you to be anything *but* on the level. Ain't askin' you to be, don't want you to be. The most way you can help me is just to do what you should do."

"Yes?"

"I said so. This is a rough town and it's a big place, and it gets a lot of people that ain't exactly panty waists. A good tough house dick—and I know you ain't no coward, whatever else you been—can save trouble for me."

"Well," Bugs hesitated troubledly. "It sounds all right. And Ford, by God, it has to be! If I got into just one more jam—"

"Sure," Ford cut in soothingly, "you just can't do it. A fella in your spot has to do everything he can to keep out of trouble, because he ain't got too many chances left."

"And you think I can handle the job, a guy that—that acts like I do? I don't mean I don't act all right, get me?" Bugs added hastily. "I give just as good as I get. But I won't take any guff from anyone—and I don't give a hoot in hell who they are either. And I won't go around with a big possum grin on my face—"

"Yeah, sure, I understand," Ford nodded. "You ain't going to do no getting along with no one. It's up to them to get along with you."

"That's not what I said! What I said was that—" Bugs scowled, then his face twisted into a sheepish grin. "I guess it did sound that way," he said mildly. "I guess that's probably the way it is."

"Or been," Ford corrected. "You live like a man should for a while, get yourself some reason for livin', and you'll feel a lot different. Well"—he got up from the desk—"guess we're all set, huh? Let me run up and get my hat and coat, and we'll be on our way."

He left. Bugs got up and paced nervously around the room. As attractive as this set-up seemed, in some ways, he was worried about it. Suspicious of Ford. Ford's clownish mannerisms were too exaggerated, no more than a mask for a coldly calculating and super-sharp mind. He wouldn't go to these lengths simply to place an efficient house detective in the Hanlon Hotel.

Still—Bugs thought—how could he be so sure? He didn't think like an ordinary man any more; he'd reached the point where he was suspicious of everyone. Ford was on the take, of course, but you found graft just about everywhere. And aside from that, and his treatment of the girl, Amy . . .

Bugs frowned, remembering. Firmly, he removed her from his calculations about Ford. Maybe she was asking for that kind of treatment. *But she wasn't, she couldn't be!* At any rate, she was none of his business.

Bugs paused in front of the old fieldstone fireplace, studying the several pictures which stood propped on the mantel. There was one of a young boy—Ford, obviously—standing beside a collie dog. There was one of a spade-bearded, bespectacled man, and another of an exotic-looking, proud-eyed brunette in a high-necked shirtwaist. There was—the remaining picture had toppled over. Bugs picked it up, and stared into the face of the girl, Amy.

Her lips were parted slightly. Her eyes looked straight into his; smiling, dancing with happy expectancy. Pleased with herself and him, and delighted that life had brought two such nice people together.

And from right behind him, Ford coughed.

Bugs jumped. He dropped the picture back to the mantel. "Hope you don't mind," he mumbled. "I was just, uh—"

"Aw, now, sure not," Ford drawled. "You don't see a dawg like that very often. He was the first and last dawg I ever had. Just seemed like I couldn't never find another one to measure up to him after he passed on."

"I see. Uh—those are your parents?"

"Yep. Fine-looking woman, ain't she? Traced her ancestry clear back to the Con-kee-stadors. Let's see, now"— Ford waggled his cigar thoughtfully. "I guess it was right after that dawg picture was taken that she run off with a cattle buyer."

Bugs didn't know what to say to that. Nor to the deputy's next statement that his mother was one helluva smart woman. "Didn't try to do what she wasn't made to." But he felt that Ford had said a great deal to him.

"Now, that little gal there," Ford went on. "That's my fee-an-say, Amy Standish. Teaches school here in town. Probably do a lot better some place else, but she's lived here all her life and her family before her for God knows how long. So it looks like I'm stuck with her."

"Your're *stuck!*" Bugs turned on him. "I'd say you were damned lucky!"

"Well, now, I guess you would," Ford nodded, "just seein' her in that old picture. But she's got fat as a hawg since it was taken."

"Fat? Why, you're—" Reddening, Bugs choked off the sentence.

Ford looked at him innocently. "Yeah? You was sayin', McKenna?"

"Nothing. Are we going to stand here talking all day, or are we going to see about that job?"

"Just as soon as I make a phone call," Ford said. "Want to do me a little favor while you're waitin'? There's a sign out there on the door—keep forgettin' to take it down—an' if you'll get a screwdriver out of the—"

"Do it yourself!" Bugs grunted. "I'll wait for you in the car."

He slammed out of the house and climbed into the convertible. A couple of minutes later, Ford joined him. He had a fresh cigar in his mouth. He was wearing a coat that matched his blue serge trousers, and a tan ranch-style hat.

"Couldn't reach Mrs. Hanlon at the hotel," he announced, as he headed the car toward town. "Have to look around a little for her."

"All right," Bugs said.

"Now, I been thinkin'—got an idea I better fix you up with a gun for your job. Don't figure you'll have any call to use it, but sometimes the best way of not needin' one is to have it."

"Yeah?" Bugs said. "What about yourself?"

"Oh, well, me, now . . ." Ford paused to turn the car into the curb. "That's a different situation. Me, I'm never around any action. Never run into nothing where a gun might be necessary."

He had parked at the end of the old town's main street, the beginning of the boom town's chief thoroughfare. They walked to the end of it, then crossed in the deep reddish dust, and started back up the plank sidewalk on the other side.

Mammoth sixteen-wheeled trucks lumbered down the street toward the oilfields. The smell of white-corn whiskey drifted from doorways. There was an incessant tinkling of juke-boxes, a clang-clinking of slot machines, the rattle-and-smack of dice and the whirr-and-click of roulette wheels. The noise rose and fell, a chorus that faded with the passing of one doorway and picked up, in perfect tempo and tune, at the next.

There were no "women." None, at least, who appeared to be anything but women (no quotes). So Ford apparently did draw the line somewhere. The men were young, not-so-young, but never old. Most of them wore hats spattered with drill-mud, and the "rattlesnake insurance" of laced eighteen-inch boots.

Ford paused at each establishment and glanced inside. Near the end of the second block, he looked over the swinging doors of a gambling house, and gave Bugs a nod of satisfaction.

"In here," he said, taking a pair of black kid gloves from his pocket.

He began putting them on, smoothing them over his tapering, delicate-looking fingers. A man came hurrying through the swinging doors, a burly, pasty-faced man with a slit for a mouth and eyes that were like tiny black buttons.

"Well, Lou!" he smirked nervously. "Saw you lookin' inside. Nothing wrong, is there?"

Ford didn't answer him. He didn't look up from pulling on his gloves.

"Lou. Be reasonable, huh, keed?" There was desperation in the guy's voice. "I didn't know she was in there. I swear I didn't! I just this moment came back from eatin', and I told those jerks I got working for me a thousand times not to let her—"

Bugs didn't see the blow, or, rather, two blows, that Ford delivered. They were so unexpected and executed so swiftly that he saw little more than their results . . . The man bent double suddenly, gasping for breath, ropish food spouting from his mouth. The man spinning ludicrously, spin-staggering off of the curb and collapsing in the street.

Ford brushed his gloves, one against the palm of the other. He went through the twin swinging doors, and immediately two chairs crashed out through the windows.

Bugs blinked and shook his head. Customers were stampeding out the doorway, but he lunged through them and past them to the inside. Again, he could hardly believe what he saw.

Ford was strolling toward the rear of the room, leaving a shambles of broken furniture and fixtures behind him, adding to it with every step he took. He moved unhurriedly, effortlessly; he was completely unruffled and the cigar was still in his teeth. And yet he gave the impression of raging, barely controllable fury. It came from the very deliberation of his movements, perhaps: a feeling that he was building up, relishing and prolonging the savagery, forestalling the cataclysmic climax that would end his game.

A couple of the joint's employees rushed him, one from each side. Ford rocked them with two simultaneous backhands, whipped his arms around their necks and crashed their heads together.

And he hardly seemed to break stride. He was moving on before they hit the floor, tipping his hat politely to a woman who stood pressed against the rear wall.

She was the last customer in the place, the only remaining person aside from Bugs and Ford. An ash-blonde, she had a kind of washed-out but interesting prettiness; full, high breasts, and a waist approximately half the circumference of her hips.

"Now, that was a hell of a thing to do!" she said angrily. "Honestly, Lou Ford! I—I—could just absolutely murder you!"

"Told you to keep out of these joints," Ford said. "Told 'em to keep you out."

"And just who are you to order me around? Where do you get off at telling me what to do with my own money?"

"But it ain't your own," Ford said gently. "Might not be none of your own either, if you got hard-pressed and had to start grabbin'. No, sir, sure might not be, and that's a fact."

The woman looked at him sulkily. "Well," she said. "Well, anyway, you didn't need to act like *this!*"

"No?" Ford shrugged. "Well, maybe not. But, look—I want you to meet a fella . . . Mrs. Hanlon, Mr. McKenna."

Her eyes swept Bugs contemptuously, taking in the worn clothes, the run-down shoes, the tired haggard face. Then she reddened, for far from flinching, she found Bugs looking her over in exactly the same way; adding her up point by point, and arriving at an obviously unflattering total.

"*Well!*" she said, unconsciously sucking in her breath. And then she smiled suddenly and extended her hand. "I'm very glad to meet you, Mr.—Mr. McKenna, is it?"

"Yeah. That's right, Mrs.—Mrs. Hanlon?"

He grinned at her insolently. But Joyce Hanlon refused to be offended. She moved in on him, clinging to his hand, until her breasts were almost against his body. She looked up at him through silky eyelashes, spoke in the voice of a plaintive child.

"I'm sorry. Don't be mad, hmmm? Pretty please? Pretty please with sugar on it?"

Bugs had no defense for that kind of stuff. He turned six different colors at once; mumbled desperately that s-sure, he wasn't angry and he hoped she wasn't and he was sorry, too, and—and so on, until he was sure he must sound like the world's biggest horse's ass.

At last Ford rescued him with the suggestion that they get out of the place. Go somewhere they could talk. They went to one of the old-town restaurants, with Joyce holding to Bugs's arm. And strangely it didn't fluster him much now. When she sat down in the booth opposite him and Ford, he missed the pressure on his biceps, the intimate, secretive probing of her fingers.

A waitress brought coffee. Ford brought up the subject of the house dick's job, stating Bugs's qualifications along with a casual mention of his criminal record.

"Plenty husky and gutsy. Been a big-city dick. An' like you can see, he's a real friendly fella to boot. Shouldn't ought to matter much that he's done a few things that wasn't exactly legal."

"It shouldn't?" Joyce looked at him doubtfully. "I mean, well, no, it shouldn't. It certainly wouldn't matter to me, I know. But . . ."

She stared, frowning, into Ford's eyes, seeking some clue

to his reasoning. The deputy looked back at her blandly. "Well, it won't matter to Mis-ter Hanlon, then," he said. "People's all alike, the way I figger. All kind of brothers under the skin."

"Oh, Lou! You corny so-and-so. But seriously—"

"Ain't never been nothin' but serious. I'm one of these Pag-lee-atchee fellas, serious as all hell behind a mask of laughter. So you just do like I say. Take Bugs, Mr. McKenna, here, right to the head man, so's he don't get lost or strayed in the application-blank stage. And Mis-ter Hanlon'll sign him up as fast as fox-hair."

"I don't think so. The mere fact that I want him hired will be enough to get him turned down. I'm perfectly willing to do it, Bugs"—she used the nickname easily, slanting a smile at him—"but I know how Mike is."

Bugs nodded uncomfortably. He started to say that they could forget the whole thing as far as he was concerned: he didn't want to be pushed off on anyone. But Ford was already talking:

"Seems to me you *don't* know how he is," he said. "Or what he is. Hard-headed. Long-shot player. Can't run his own game, he'll tackle the other fella's, try to take the play away from him. That's your husband, honey, and I don't figger he'll step out of character with Bugs."

"Mmm, yes. I see what you mean." She took a thoughtful sip of her coffee and pushed the cup aside. "I think you're right, Lou. Now, do I mention that I met Bugs through you, or—?"

"It's up to you, but it don't make much difference. He'd probably think it, even if you didn't tell him."

"And don't you know it! Trust him not to give anyone the benefit of the doubt!"

"Well, doubts is cheap these days," Ford said. "Goin' at the same rate as their benefits, which was nothing-minus the last I heard." He slid out of the booth and stood up. "Guess I better run along, now that we're all squared away. Some fellas I know are leavin' town, and I want to give 'em a send-off."

"Have fun," Joyce smiled and flirted a hand at him. "I'll let you know how everything comes out."

"And thanks," Bugs said gruffly. "Thanks a lot."

"What for? Ain't done nothin' to call for thanks," Ford declared. "No, sir, I sure ain't. And that's a fact."

Most of the Hanlon employees worked the more or less standard long-day, short-day of the hotel world. A shift came on duty at seven in the morning, quit at noon, returned at six and remained until eleven. The following day, this shift would work a short-day—from noon until six—with the opposite shift catching the double-watch long day.

The exceptions to this routine were night workers, certain professional and maintenance personnel, employees of the store-room and laundry, Bugs McKenna, and Mr. Olin Westbrook, the executive manager. Bugs was on call at all times. But there was rarely any need for him during the day—he had been called only once during the month of his employment—so, in practice, he was a night worker. Mr. Olin Westbrook, on the other hand, not only was *supposed* to be available at all hours of the day, but invariably had to be.

Oh, perhaps he could retire to a checked-out room for an hour or so. Freshen up with a shower, or catch a few winks of sleep. But these brief periods were more tantalizing than satisfying; he couldn't really rest and relax. If someone didn't buzz him—and someone usually did—he would be expecting them to. And the expectation, coupled with the worry over what might be going on during his absence, kept him on nerve ends.

Westbrook was a hotel man of the old school, of the days when it was a pleasure to stop at a hotel instead of an adventure into indifferent food and accommodations, insolently or ignorantly administered. Now, at the Hanlon, he tried to do too much with too pitifully little. The job might be killing him, but he had to have it. He was in his late fifties, and for the last ten years he had been fired from every job he held. So it was this job or nothing.

. . . At eleven o'clock at night, he was in his mezzanine-floor office, re-auditing the hotel's books for the last three months. It was the third time he had been through them, and the result had been the same each time. There was a broad, fixed smile on his face: a frozen grimace. In his mind, deliberately overlaid with protective dullness, was terror.

Cold sober, Westbrook had many of the reactions of a man who is dead drunk. The direst personal catastrophe had no meaning for him. He could be face to face with a fact, yet remain completely withdrawn from it. He had been that way for years—*God, how many years?* Only when the alcoholic content of his blood was at a certain level could he think and act as he should.

At last he pushed aside the papers and took a pint bottle from his desk. It was about a third full. It was the last of three pints with which he had started the day. Westbrook drank half of it at a swallow and lighted a cigarette. After a few puffs on the cigarette, he drank the remainder. Warmth came back into his small paunchy body. His fixed, foolish smile gave way to a scowl of concentration.

Well? he thought. And then: *I don't know.*

But you've got to! It's your tail if you don't. You hired Dudley, did it over the old man's objections. You said that he was a hell of a good auditor, and you'd vouch for him personally. And now that the son-of-a-bitch has done this . . .

I know! I know all that, dammit. But I still don't know . . . Perhaps if I had another drink—And of course I'll close out the watch before I take it; get the night shift under way . . .

Mr. Westbrook stood up resolutely, ignoring a small and despairing voice of warning. Rolling down his sleeves, he refastened the links of the French cuffs and rebuttoned his fawn-colored vest. He put on a black broadcloth coat, carefully adjusting the white linen handkerchief in its breast pocket. Then, after swiftly examining his fingernails and flicking a speck of dust from one shoe, he stepped out onto the mezzanine.

Rosalie Vara, the mezz' maid, was dusting furniture a few feet away from him. Studying her from the rear, Westbrook again complimented himself for assigning her to her present duties. She would have got herself raped if he hadn't. Any girl who looked like she did—who could easily have passed for white and yet admitted to being a Negro—was obviously too stupid to look after herself. All that was necessary was opportunity, which, on the job he had given her, was practically nonexistent.

Westbrook let his eyes linger on her a moment longer, his ultra-cynical mind again considering the possibility that instead of being stupid she might be very, very smart. Considering it, and again rejecting it. She couldn't be working a gimmick. He knew every trick and dodge in the book, and if there was any way that a gal could pull a swiftie by admitting that she was a Negro . . . well, there just wasn't. She was simply dumb, that was all. Too damned dull-witted to tell a lie. So he'd put her in a job where no one could take advantage of her.

Of course, she was upstairs occasionally. It was unavoidable, since all the day maids knocked off at eleven o'clock, and there were a few rooms, like Bugs McKenna's, which had to be put in order before the morning shift came on. For ninety-five per cent of the time, however, she worked as she was working now. Out in the open. Away from the danger of private bedrooms and locked doors.

Westbrook took a final look at the girl's delicately rounded bottom; a look of unconscious yearning. Then he turned away conscientiously and descended the curving staircase to the lobby. He walked with his head tilted slightly upward, as though about to sniff the air for some evil smell. His pale puffy face was as self-assuredly haughty as that of a pure-bred Pekingese, to which it bore some slight resemblance. People were tempted to smile at their first glimpse of Westbrook. But the very briefest contact with the little man was sufficient to still the temptation. Westbrook had begun his career as a page boy. Working his way upward, he had become not only highly efficient but exceedingly tough—a man who could cope with the hurly-burly hotel world at every level and on its own terms.

The staircase terminated in the lobby near the three front elevators. Two of the cars were out of service, as they should have been at this hour. The third was being manned by a member of the day crew, which it definitely should not have been.

Westbrook glanced up the lobby to the front-office desks. He moved toward them ominously. The youngish night clerk, Leslie Eaton, was in the cashier's cage. (The clerk handled all front-office duties at night.) Chaffing with him, his back turned to the lobby, was the dayshift bell captain. Neither he nor the clerk noted Westbrook's approach. They were suddenly made aware of it by a bellowed inquiry as to what the hell was going on.

The captain jumped and whirled. Westbrook let out another bellow. "You working this shift now? Well? Are you too stupid to talk? What about you, Eaton? You were doing plenty of yapping a minute ago!"

"I—I—I'm sorry, sir," the clerk stammered. "I m-mean—"

"Been getting a lot of kicks on you. Not answering your phones. Chasing all over the house instead of staying where you belong. I know, I know"—Westbrook made a chopping motion with his hand. "You have a little auditing to do. Have to check up on the coffee-shop and the valet and so on. But that's no reason to be gone from the desk for thirty or forty minutes at a time."

"I'm not!—I mean," Eaton corrected himself, "I'm not aware that I have been absent for more than a few minutes," He was a rosy-cheeked young man addicted to college-cut clothes.

Westbrook looked at him distastefully, advised him that he was aware of it *now*, and turned back to the captain. "Well," he demanded, "where's the night bellboy? What's that day man doing on the elevator?"

"We're both working over," the captain shrugged sullenly. "Night boys haven't shown up yet."

"Why not?"

"Don't know. Look, Mr. Westbrook," the captain protested, "what are you jumping on me for? Those birds aren't on my shift."

"And aren't you tickled to death that they aren't!" Westbrook jeered. "Got you buffaloed, haven't they? Bet they're in the locker-room right now, and you haven't got the guts to run 'em up!"

The arrival of a guest ended his harangue. The captain scurried away, gratefully, to take the man's baggage. Westbrook left the lobby and started down the back stairs. The door to the bellboy's locker-room was partially open. Pausing in the dimly lit corridor, Westbrook looked through the aperture.

Like many "boys" in the hotel world, Ted and Ed Gusick, respectively the night bellboy and elevator operator, were boys in name only. Ted was about forty, Ed perhaps a year or so older. They had prematurely graying hair, and pinkish massaged-looking faces. They were well-built but slender; narrow-waisted, flat-stomached: wiry and strong. Born of the same mother, they may or may not have had the same father. Even she was unable to say. Amoral, vicious, treacherous and dishonest, they bore the hard polish of men who have spent a lifetime squeezing out of tight places.

They were fighting, standing almost toe to toe while they slugged each other. A veteran of a thousand such locker-room brawls, Westbrook watched them with a feeling of nostalgia. Every blow was intended to cripple. Anything went, except hitting the other man in the face. Boys didn't fight that way anymore, Westbrook was thinking. They didn't fight period. They came whining to the management with their disputes: always, as in every difficulty, they wanted someone to do something for them. They were incompetent, indifferent, completely lacking in pride in their work—"too good" to do the job they were paid to do.

Well . . .

Westbrook sighed, shook his head and pulled himself back from the happy past. Then, setting his face in a ferocious scowl, he dashed into the locker-room, managing, by a miracle of foot-work, to give both boys a solid kick before they could elude him.

"Up!" he roared, pointing dramatically to the ceiling. "Up on the g'damn floor! What's the matter with you, anyway? You know what time it is? What d'you mean keeping a watch waiting?"

"Sorry, sir" said Ed.

"Sorry, Mr. Westbrook," said Ted.

And they edged warily toward the door. Westbrook advanced on them, one hard little fist drawn back.

"What were you fighting about, huh? Hah? Answer me, you friggers, or I'll—"

Ted said they had been fighting about nothing. Ed said they had no excuse. These replies were exactly the right ones, in Westbrook's opinion. In the old days, boys often fought out of sheer high spirits, and they made no excuses if caught. Nevertheless, as a matter of discipline—and because they expected it—he took a vicious swing at the brothers, cursing them roundly as they fled out the door and up the stairs.

Now, those were real boys, he thought, as he left the locker-room. You'd never catch boys like that whining or complaining. They knew how to wait on a guest, to get their own way with a man and do it so ingratiatingly that he was glad to pay for the privilege. In the last twenty years, they had worked with Westbrook in perhaps a dozen different hotels. Shrewd and suave, knowing hotels from sub-basement to roof garden, they could probably have managed one as well as he. But they remained bellboys by choice. They were good at hopping bells, and it left them free of onerous responsibilities. Also—unless Westbrook missed his guess—they made more money than he did.

Ordinarily, neither of the brothers would have accepted employment as an elevator operator. One of them had done so in this case because only the night bellboy's job was open and they insisted on working together. At the time he had hired them, Westbrook had promised to give them day jobs on bells as soon as they became available. But they had later advised him not to bother, that they were completely satisfied with things as they were.

Westbrook correctly suspected that their preference for the night shift was largely due to the scanty supervision thereon. Certainly they would be able to run circles around that goofy clerk, Leslie Eaton. But no one had caught them in any forbidden activities as yet, and until someone did catch them, or at least came forth with a valid complaint . . .

Well, that was that, Westbrook shrugged. They were good boys.

The dopey dullness of sobriety was creeping back over him. He was passing out on his feet, and there was still that all-important matter of Dudley to settle.

Westbrook hurried out the back door, fighting to keep the telltale smirk from his face. When he returned, some twenty minutes later, he was once again brisk and alert. And there were two half-pints of whiskey in his pockets, and another half in his stomach.

He entered the unattended service elevator and switched on the light. He shot upward, the control pushed all the way over, arriving seconds later at the twelfth floor. It was a perfect stop, with the car exactly level with the landing. Westbrook rewarded himself with a couple of "short ones"—adding another half-pint of whiskey to his interior content.

He tossed the empty bottle into the incinerator chute. Turning away from it, he suddenly staggered wildly and flailed the air with his arms. The fit was gone almost as soon as it came: he had moved in an insane blur for a moment, and then it was all over. But Westbrook knew that it signaled the crossing of an invisible line. From now on the booze would be working against him, sweeping him finally into the dark and disastrous void which he had penetrated so often in the past.

Westbrook shivered slightly, remembering those occasions. He remembered the agony that had followed them, the terrible sickness and the equally terrible shame and embarrassment. He couldn't go through it again. *God, he couldn't do it!* He could not, must not, take another drink tonight!

Except, of course, one very small one. Just enough to see him through this Dudley matter.

He took it. He re-corked the bottle, then slowly uncorked it and took another one. Seemingly, there were no ill effects.

He did feel a rising anger, but that was natural enough. Goddammit, how long could a man go on catching the dirty end of the stick without getting fed up? He never got any rest. He never had a minute to call his own. Work, by God, that was all he ever got. Work and more work, and then still more work. And what did he have to work with, hah? A bunch of bumbling, bastardly lunatics! And was it appreciated, hah? Did he ever get a goddamned word of thanks, hah?

Shit, no!

Westbrook snapped suddenly out of his self-pitying reverie, wondering if he had spoken aloud. He decided (1) that he hadn't, (2) that he didn't give a damn if he had, and (3) that he wasn't the kind of a man who went around talking to himself. The first decision was entirely correct, the last almost. He became hatefully insulting and murderously angry when his alcoholic tolerance was exceeded. But he had to be literally saturated before he appeared drunk, in the usual sense. The fact was at once his curse and his blessing.

He drank the remainder of his whiskey. Then, with his shoulders hunched pugilistically, his eyes squinted to pinpoints, and his face flushed with righteous indignation, he stamped down the corridor. He was in a wing of the building, one of its two wings. Bugs McKenna's room was a few steps away, facing the court as did the rooms of all employees who slept in.

Westbrook strode up to the door. He drew his fist back, hesitated—held it poised for a matter of seconds—and then he pounded.

Bugs had been awakened by the ringing of the telephone. It was his usual eleven p.m. wake-up call, and he and the operator exchanged the usual amenities. With that out of the way, she advised him that yes, he had had one call.

"Mrs. Hanlon. She said you could give her a ring whenever you waked up."

"Oh," Bugs said. "Well, thanks."

"Yes, sir. Shall I get her for you now, sir?"

Bugs didn't like the tone of her voice, the subtle note of amusement. So he said, "No. I'll tell you when I want you to call her," and slammed up the receiver.

He took a shower. Toweling his big body, he decided that he was jumping at shadows again, acting like a touchy kid instead of a man. He was wrong about the telephone operator. Or, if he wasn't—if she was a little tickled about Mrs. Hanlon's almost nightly calls—what of it? It was nothing to get sore about. He should have let her have her little joke and pretended not to notice.

"Got to watch that stuff," he murmured aloud. "You've

been getting along swell, so don't start slipping."

He shaved. He dressed, standing in front of the door-length mirror, and unconsciously, contentedly, he began to hum. He looked like a different man these days. More important, he felt like one. He was still unsure of himself, still inclined to jump down people's throats for little or no cause, but not nearly to the extent he had used to be. All the old, ugly impulses were vanishing or becoming atrophied. Withering in these strange new feelings of security, an environment which asked no more than he could decently give.

The Hanlon had no interests whatsoever in its guests' morals. Its concern was not so much with what they did, but how they did it. As long as they were circumspect, they could do anything they chose to within reason. It was only when they became rowdy, or otherwise acted to the hotel's disadvantage, that McKenna was called in.

It wasn't that way everywhere, according to Olin Westbrook. In many big hotels, the house dick had to be a keyhole-peeper, a sneak and a snoop. Otherwise, his employers would get a reputation for running a loose house, and the trade would go to their competition. But the Hanlon had no competition, nor would it ever have any. So it could rock along in the easy-going style of its area. And Bugs McKenna had to do nothing offensive to his self-respect.

He heard the rattle of silver as a coffee tray was set down outside his door. Bringing it in, he took it over by the window, sniffing its steam happily as he filled a cup. Now, this was something like it, he thought. To live in a nice place—be treated just about the same as a paying guest—and get paid for doing it.

Of course, Joyce Hanlon was kind of a nuisance. Just a little too interested in how he was getting along, too friendly for comfort. On the other hand, it was a lot better for her to be that way—he guessed—than uninterested and unfriendly. And, anyway, nothing was perfect.

He wasn't kicking a bit, Bugs McKenna wasn't. No, sir, not one little bit. He was satisfied with things just like they were. Later on, perhaps, he might want something more out of life than he had now. But for the present . . .

A slight frown crept into his eyes. Doggedly, he pushed away the thought that had prompted it. The present—that was all that mattered. Maintaining the status quo, and doing nothing that might endanger it. As, surely, it would be endangered by taking an active interest in Amy Standish.

She was Lou Ford's girl, Ford was obviously a thoroughly bad egg. So for the present, until he was a lot better established than he was now, he would have to leave her alone.

No damned good anyway, Bugs thought bitterly. And knew that he didn't really think it. *A swell girl like that, and she throws herself away on a—a—*

Bugs severed his chain of thought again. Firmly and finally. Lou Ford had done him a favor. Thus far, there was no indication that there was any string attached to it. He was in the deputy's debt, in other words, and it was only decent—as well as smart—to keep the fact in mind.

He drank half the coffee and smoked a couple of cigarettes. Then, he took the cup and saucer into the bathroom and washed and dried them. He had just finished when Rosalie Vara, the maid, arrived.

"How are you tonight, Mr. McKenna?" She came in smiling, a dream come to life in her neat blue-and-white uniform. "I hope you slept well."

"Not too bad, Rosie"—McKenna gestured toward the coffee tray. "Sent up more than I could drink tonight. Welcome to have it if you want it."

"Why, thank you! That's very nice of you, Mr. McKenna."

"S'all right," Bugs said. "No sense in letting good coffee go to waste."

He was conscious that he had used these same words, gone through this same rigamarole, practically every night since he came here. But the fact didn't bother him, as it would have with another person. Nor was he anything but pleased by her warmly gentle laugh, a laugh which told him that she saw through his gruffness. He felt at ease with her, as he had never felt with anyone else. Probably, he supposed, because she was so completely at ease herself.

She finished the coffee, Bugs idled near the window while she made up his room, wondering why such a swell-looking girl—who could easily have passed for white—should have declared herself a Negro. It wasn't because she was stupid, as Westbrook said. She was obviously smarter, and better educated, than most of the Hanlon's white employees. Neither was it because of the aggressive arrogance which Bugs had found in so many Negros, and which had always made him so excruciatingly uncomfortable around them. They—that type of Negro—hit you in the face with their color. They drew a line, then despised you if you came over to their side and hated you if you stayed on your own. Rosalie Vara, on the other hand . . .well, Rosie was just herself. An exceptionally pretty and nice-mannered young woman who happened to be a Negro, and who saw no reason either to flaunt or conceal the fact.

"Well"—she picked up her work bucket and cleaning equipment—"it looks like I'm all through, Mr. McKenna. Thanks again for the coffee."

"Not at all. Thank *you*," Bugs said. "Well, guess I'll probably run into you later on tonight, huh?"

"Yes, sir. 'Bye, now, Mr. McKenna."

She left, her small round hips swinging. A few minutes later, as Bugs was preparing to leave, Olin Westbrook pounded on the door.

Bugs opened it. The manager pushed past him brusquely, seated himself, and pointed imperiously to a chair in front of him. "Sit down. Sit *down*, I said! I've got some things to say to you, and it's going to take a little time."

"Well, sure, Ollie . . ." Bugs sat down. "What's on your mind?"

"I'll tell you. But I've got a question to ask first. What do you think of me, personally, that is? Think I'm on the square? Got any kicks about the way I've treated you since you've been here?"

"Why do you ask that?" Bugs looked at him frowning. "Has anyone said that—?"

"Just answer me, dammit! You came here green as a gourd. Have I or have I not done everything that a man could do to put you on the right track and keep you there?"

"You have. No one could have been more helpful, and I've tried to tell you how much I appreciate it. Now—"

"Then you do owe me a favor? I helped you when you needed it, and I'm not out of line in asking you to help me now?"

"That's right." Bugs nodded curiously. "Look, Ollie. Let's lay it on the line. I'm going to be pretty short until payday, but you can have what I've got. And if there's anything else that I—"

"It's something else. It's Dudley—you know, the auditor. He's my baby. I hired him over the old man's objections. All right. Hanlon was right about him. In the last quarter, Dudley's knocked down more than five thousand dollars. Between five and six—I can't say exactly how much. I want you to get it back from him."

"Me?" Bugs gave a start. "Oh, you mean you want me to put him under arrest. Turn him over to the cops and file a complaint—"

"No! I don't mean that, because I can't prove he's stolen it. I know he has, understand. We've done just as much business this quarter as we did last, but we've got five or six thousand less to show for it. So—"

"But—but how—" Bugs was beginning to see where the conversation was drifting, and it frightened him stiff. "But—"

"What's the difference how? There's a thousand and one ways an auditor can knock down. He can't do it in a place where there's other auditors, a system of checks and rechecks. But—" Westbrook flung up his hand in exasperation. "Look. Hotel books are kept in pencil!—the transcript sheets, the cash sheets, everything. They have to be because they're running accounts. New charges being added all the time. Erasures, and changes are taken as a matter of course. All right, then—just to give you one trick for knocking down. A guest checks in one night. He doesn't leave until after our check-out period the following night, so naturally we charge him for two days. But in hours, he's actually only been here one day, and by altering his folio and the cash sheet—Yes?"

"Nothing," Bugs said nervously. "I mean, I was just going to say that if you can't prove something—if you aren't absolutely positive—"

"I told you I was positive, dammit! I know that he took that dough, and Hanlon will know it. And he'll hold me responsible."

"But—but how did he get away with so much? Why

didn't you stop him when he first started knocking down?"

"It's not something you can spot on a daily check. The loss isn't big enough. But when it collects over a period of three months . . .!" Westbrook scrubbed his face irritably. "Would I be kidding you?" he demanded. "Don't you think I know what I'm talking about?"

"No, of course, not." Bugs shook his head, he nodded it. "But—"

"Dudley took that dough. He wouldn't have banked it or put it in a safety deposit box. It might cause talk, and anyway he'd want it where he could get to it in a hurry. So he's got it with him, either in his room or on his person. He's probably changed it into a handful of big bills, and . . ." Westbrook's voice faded suddenly. He choked and coughed, stared at Bugs out of desperately belligerent eyes. "You've got to get it back, Bugs. Scare hell out of him. Slap him around, beat him up if you have to. *But get it back!*"

It was what Bugs had expected. And he had known what he was going to have to do. But still it was hard to do it. He liked Ollie Westbrook. Few people had been as kind to him as the stiff-necked, haughty-mannered little manager.

"Let's see what you're asking of me, Ollie," he said quietly. "You can't recover the loss through the bonding company, right? They're in the same boat with you. They can't prove that any dough he may have isn't his own. And you can't prove it either."

"But, goddammit, where would a guy like that get five or six grand? How can he prove it's his?"

"He doesn't have to. He doesn't have to say where he got it. So—" Bugs spread his hands. "That's how we stand, Ollie. I've got a criminal record, a damned ugly one. One wrong move, and I'm in the soup up to my neck. And yet you're asking me to pull a robbery, an act of extortion. To take a man's money—and it is *his*, in the eyes of the law—by force and violence . . . I don't believe you've thought this thing through, Ollie. I don't really think you want me to take a chance like that. Or do you?"

Westbrook hesitated. Then, shamed but dogged, he said it was exactly what he wanted. And expected. "I mean, I want you to get that dough back. Make him come across. You're not taking any chances. A bastard like that isn't going to make trouble for anyone."

"He won't for me, anyway." Bugs shook his head firmly. "I'm grateful to you, Ollie, but I think you've got a hell of a lot of guts. You're afraid to tackle this deal yourself, yet you'll ask me—a guy walking a tight rope—and—"

"Afraid, hell!" Westbrook exploded. "I'd take on fifty skunks like Dudley if it would do any good. But it wouldn't! I insisted on hiring him. I swore that he was straight as a string. How can I do an about-face now and call him a thief? He'd laugh in my face. I'd just be tipping him off that it was time to scram. You see that, don't you? You're not completely dumb, are you, you overgrown meathead?"

McKenna colored. He said coldly, "Not *this* dumb, at least. I'm sorry, Ollie."

"You won't do it? After all I've done for you, you—"

"I won't do it," Bugs nodded. "And I'll be damned careful not to accept any other favors from you from now on."

Westbrook brushed the back of his hand against his mouth. He said, hell, he was sorry; he didn't want Bugs to feel that way. He hadn't done anything more for Bugs than he'd do for any man that he liked, and Bugs didn't owe him a cent. But—but—

His voice rose, turned suddenly ugly. The alcohol washed over him like a tide, killing all inhibitions, leaving nothing but his terror and sense of outrage. And hateful words spewed from his small hard mouth in a poisonous stream.

He didn't mean what he said. It was the alcohol talking, not the man. But he was inherently cynical, gifted with the faculty for totting circumstance with circumstance and arriving at invariably unflattering conclusions. Conclusions—answers—which were at once laughably illogical and insidiously convincing.

Bugs gaped at him, not knowing whether to laugh or get sore.

The reddish haze cleared from Westbrook's brain, and his tirade ended as abruptly as it had begun. He got to his feet, stood weaving on them slightly murmuring dull-voiced apologies.

He was sorry . . .just lost his temper . . .worried and

burned up about Dudley, and—that was all. He hadn't meant a word of it . . .

"Well, Christ," Bugs frowned, "I should hope not."

"Sure, not. Not a word." Westbrook tottered toward the door. "So just forget it, huh? Enough trouble now without . . ."

The door closed behind him.

Bugs stared at its polished surface, a sickish disturbance spreading through the pit of his stomach.

He was supposed to bump off old man Hanlon? That was why Joyce Hanlon and Lou Ford had done so much string-pulling to get him this job?

Nuts! How crazy could you get, anyway? Still, if that wasn't the reason behind Ford's and Joyce's unusual interest in him—and, of course, it wasn't, what . . .?

Well, it was like Ford had said. A good tough house-dick at the Hanlon saved work for him and his deputies. *But that wasn't true. Nothing had happened at the Hanlon thus far that required any great amount of toughness or muscular activity.*

So? Well, so nothing. Perhaps things had just been unusually quiet so far. Or, well, maybe Ford had just been doing him a favor in a way that would be easy for him to accept. That last didn't seem very likely, but . . .

Ford was a grafter, a crook. And Joyce Hanlon was obviously pretty low-down. The two of them were both money-hungry. And if they were looking for a guy to pull a murder, what could be more natural than to pick someone who'd—?

Bugs let out a disgusted snort, a sound filled with forced disbelief. He told himself that just because Ollie Westbrook was acting screwy was no excuse for him to do so. Ford and Joyce knew that he was on the level. He'd made it damned clear that he was, and that he intended to stay that way. And if they'd actually been looking for a killer, he wouldn't have got the job.

That was that. Poor Ollie had just been grasping at straws, saying the first thing that popped into his mind.

Bugs slipped on his shoulder holster, with its .38 Police Special. Then, putting on his hat and coat, he left the room.

He was supposed to make a complete tour of the hotel at least once a night. Tonight, as he sometimes did, he decided to make part of it before eating, and the rest afterwards.

Since he was here, he did his own floor first, walking the main hall and the two wing corridors. Then, mounting the two flights of steps to the fourteenth—the top—floor, he began working his way downward.

To save doubling back on his tracks, he descended the east-wing steps on one floor, those on the west wing the next. In this fashion, he arrived some twenty minutes later on the eleventh floor . . .at the room of the auditor, Dudley.

He had been thinking about Westbrook, meanwhile. Worrying about him. Fretting himself into a state of stricken conscience. He'd acted like a heel, he decided. Just turned the little man down flat without a crumb of comfort. Naturally, he couldn't go to the lengths that Westbrook had suggested, but there was every chance in the world that they wouldn't be necessary. Westbrook was too rattled to think straight, to suggest anything but threats and violence. Whereas, if the auditor actually was a thief, he might easily knuckle under to a few firm words.

At any rate, Bugs thought, there was no harm in trying. And he certainly owed it to Westbrook to make the try.

So, impulsively, without stopping to listen at the door— and, God, how he was to regret that later!—he knocked briskly.

There was silence. The kind of silence that follows the sudden cessation of sound. Bugs waited a moment, and knocked again.

Still silence. Then, a sudden creak and rattle, the brisk chatter of the bathroom shower. And Dudley's irritated voice.

"Yeah? Who is it?"

"McKenna," Bugs said. "I want to see you."

"This time of night? What the hell, Bugs?"

Bugs didn't say anything. Dudley muttered something and turned the key in the lock, stepping into the bathroom as Bugs entered. "Be right with you," he called sourly. "Just as soon as I dry off, and get . . ."

He slammed the door, cutting off the last of the sentence. Bugs went on through the entrance areaway and sat down. Except for the moonlight drifting through the window drapes, the room lay in darkness. The bed was rumpled as though slept in. Dudley's clothes were flung over a chair. Or, rather, part of them were. The trousers, with the belt half-pulled out of them, lay on the floor in an untidy heap.

Bugs looked at them, frowning unconsciously. That was funny. Dudley was kind of a lady's man. A real dude about his clothes. It was strange that he'd drop them on the floor in a wad, as strange, say, as his getting out of bed in the middle of the night to take a bath . . .

The bathroom door opened. A figure darted past him suddenly. Dudley, his hair rumpled, naked save for the towel tied around his middle. He snatched up the trousers, clawed frantically at the inside surface of the belt. He dropped them again and turned on Bugs, eyes glittering in the darkness, teeth bared in an animal-like grimace.

"All right," he hissed. "Let's have it, you son-of-a-bitch!"

"Huh?" Bugs scrambled from his chair. "What the hell are you—"

"It's mine. You can't prove that it isn't. I know the law, see, and you either fork it over or—*or by God, I'll kill you!*"

The words came out in a rush. He came at Bugs with a rush. And hell, he was a set-up for Bugs, a flabby, wild-swinging punk like that.

Bugs side-stepped expertly, effortlessly. As the auditor shot past him, he chopped his hand against the back of his neck. "Now, simmer down," he warned, turning. "I don't know what—what—"

He stopped talking. There was no one to talk to. There were only the soles of Dudley's bare feet on the window sill . . . and then they were no longer there. They had slid over it, following his body through the fluttering drapes.

Into the eleven-story void of space.

ed Gusick set down his load of baggage and turned to the cross, dyspeptic-looking guest. In hushed, funereal tones, he advised the gentleman that the house doctor was on call at all times, and that the corner drugstore had twenty-four hour prescription service.

"Of course, you may be all right here," he said on a note of hopeful worriment. "A lot of people—the really rugged types, you know—it hardly bothers 'em at all. But if you *should* feel yourself getting sick. . ."

The man stared at him nervously. He asked worried questions. Dolefully, Ted declined to reply.

"I guess I've said too much already, sir. After all, I've got a big family to support, and if I lost my job. . ." He hesitated, then threw in the clincher. "Probably I wouldn't have said anything at all if you hadn't been double-rated. That was just a little more than I could take. To charge you a double rate for a room like this, this room above *all* rooms. . ."

"What? That clerk charged me double, you said?" Anger was added to the man's nervousness. "What's all this about, anyway? What's wrong with this room?"

Ted wouldn't tell him. He just couldn't, as much as he wanted to and felt that he should. He was just scraping by, see, and he was too old to get another job. And—

"Oh, thank you, sir," he said smoothly, pocketing the guest's five-dollar tip. "Now, don't let on that I told you, but they call this the dead room. I guess it's something in the wallpaper, know what I mean? Arsenic or something like that. Anyway, practically everyone that stays in it gets sick as a dog, and quite a few of 'em have died. So if you'll take my advice. . ."

He left as the guest was acting on his advice; i.e., he had Leslie Eaton, the clerk, on the phone, and was demanding another room . . . "a decent room, by God," he concluded furiously. "And don't try to gyp me on the price either."

Thoroughly bewildered, the clerk agreed to a transfer. Ted accepted another key from him, moved the gentleman to a room less desirable than the first one, and collected a tip of another dollar.

The next guest to arrive was flushed faced, jaundiced of eye. After considerable sly coaxing, and a ten-dollar tip, Ted revealed to him that there were indeed a great many "girls" in the hotel.

"The clerk's got a whole stable of 'em. Some of the hottest babes you ever laid eyes on. Now, don't let on that I told you because he gets kind of embarrassed about it. But just tell him you know damned well he's got 'em—you been hearing about it all over Texas—and that if he don't come across, the old crap's going to fly . . ."

The gentleman licked his lips. He reached for the telephone, and Ted made his exit. Arriving at the elevator bank, he found Ed waiting for him.

"Let's have your passkey." His brother spoke impatiently. "Old man Reimers just came in fried to the gills."

"Forget him. If he's really fried, he hasn't got any dough left."

"Says who? How the hell do you know so much? Give me that key or I'll paste you one!"

Ted stepped into the car. He pulled the door shut, gesturing his brother into silence. "No key," he said. "I got rid of it. I dropped in on Dudley a while ago, and after I made the hit . . ."

He named the figure he had hit for. Ed let out an admiring whistle. "Dudley, for Christ's sake! Must have tapped the till, don't y'suppose? How'd you ever get wise that he was carrying heavy?"

"Didn't." Ted shrugged modestly. "Didn't even know it was his room until I got inside. Well, I knew, sure, but I wasn't even thinking about whose room it was. I heard the shower running as I passed by, and I could tell by the sound that the bathroom door was closed. So naturally I paid him a fast visit."

"Naturally." Ed opened the door at the lobby floor. "A chance like that, you don't get every day . . . Well, what d'you know"—he chuckled dryly. "So Dudley gets cleaned while he's getting clean!"

"I figure that isn't all he got. I wouldn't say for sure but I got a hunch there was someone in the bathroom with him. It kind of figures, see? Otherwise, he'd've had the door open. You have it closed with the shower on, and you practically get drowned in the steam."

Ed nodded wisely. Entertaining a lady guest in the bathroom, with the water running, was one of the very oldest of tricks. It was poor for neatness, as the saying was, but perfect for secrecy.

Ted returned to the front office and went behind the key rack. Seating himself in the open window of the air well, he lighted a cigarette; relaxed, grinning, as he listened to Eaton's high-pitched voice. He was talking to that ruddy-faced guy, apparently, the last one that registered. And the guy obviously—as Ted had advised him—was refusing to take no for an answer.

". . . you listen to me, sir! I do not have any girls! I do NOT! . . . Well, I don't care . . . All I've got to say is that they're just a bunch of nasty old liars, and they ought to be ashamed of themselves and—What? What? Don't you talk to me that way, thir!"—excitement was bringing out Eaton's lisp. "I thimply will not lithen one more minute to thith—thith—"

He banged up the telephone. Chuckling softly, Ted flicked his cigarette out the window. And then, as his eyes followed its course to the bottom of the shaft, he emitted a startled curse.

He sat staring downward for a moment. His stomach churning queasily, a faint chill gripping his hard wiry body. But he had seen suicides before—leapers, like this one. And Dudley, thief and chiseler that he was bound to be, was certainly no great loss to the world.

Ted slid from the window sill and lighted another cigarette. He dropped it to the floor, emerged from behind the key rack, and joined Eaton in the room-desk cage. The clerk was still indignant from his talk with the ruddy-faced man. He told Ted about it, his voice cracking and squeaking, announcing his conviction that the gentleman was plain raving mad.

Ted nodded soberly. "It's this weather," he said. "You take a night like this, if people got any mental weakness at all, they blow their lids like bedbugs."

Eaton giggled cautiously. "Oh, you! What's so different about the weather tonight?"

"You ain't noticed?" Ted shook his head. "Well, I guess you wouldn't. But if you were an old-time hotel man, you'd know this was nut weather. The kind of night when people go sailing out their windows like airplanes."

"Oh, sure!" Eaton giggled again. "Now, what are you up to, you crazy thing?"

"No kid, kid. Why, I'll lay you ten to one we have a suicide tonight."

Eaton laughed ecstatically. Ted took him by the elbow, led him to the air-well window and pointed.

The clerk looked out. He fainted. Leaving him lying on the floor, Ted picked up the telephone.

He called Westbrook's room first. There was no answer, which was as he had expected, since, by this time of night, the manager would be pretty thoroughly anaesthetized with alcohol.

Ted jiggled the receiver hook, and called Bugs McKenna.

When Bugs thought about that night later, everything seemed to move in the hazy yet well-defined grooves of a dream. He had committed murder, yet he had not committed it. It was something of the moment, something that would have no meaning once the moment was gone. Similarly, he was in dire danger, yet none at all. The means for extricating himself were ridiculously obvious: as easily and immediately accessible as those in a clumsily constructed story.

Even after Lou Ford came on the scene,—entered the dream, there was no rift in the smooth haziness. Ford, in fact, proved its happy culmination . . . A suicide, huh? Well, now, wasn't that somethin'! Must've been an awful nice fella too, y'know, gettin' hisself all cleaned up before he did it . . .

Ford wasn't at all suspicious. He had no reason to be—and almost every reason not to be—and Bugs was sure that he wasn't. Later, within a few brief days—But that was later.

Taking things as they happened:

Bugs stared at the still-fluttering curtains of the window, and a black and terrible sickness engulfed him. He had killed Dudley. For the second time in his life, he had killed a man. He hadn't meant to; it was an accident. But he had done it, and for a moment he wanted to die himself.

The moment passed. The blackness and the sickness went away. Fear gripped him, shook him back into his senses. Shattering his regrets before they were fully formed.

Dudley was no good. Dudley had brought about his own death. He had betrayed Westbrook, a man who had befriended him, and indirectly the betrayal had cost him his life.

As to what had happened to the money that Dudley had stolen, and which he apparently believed had been stolen from him, Bugs did no thinking at all about that. Not at the time, he didn't. He simply got out of the room fast, as soon as he had ascertained that the hall was clear. He was out the door almost as soon as Dudley was out the window. Racing up the stairs. Bursting into his own room, and picking up the telephone. Speaking with a yawn in his voice:

"McKenna. Guess I fell asleep again after you called me. What time is it? . . . That late, huh? Well, maybe you better try Mrs. Hanlon for me anyhow."

She had been asleep, she said; and she was a little slow about answering the telephone. Bugs apologized for waking her up, and she said it was okay but she hadn't really wanted to see him about anything important, so why didn't he give her a ring tomorrow? Bugs said he would, and they hung up.

So that took care of that. He hadn't left his room at the time of Dudley's death. Or, at least, he had been in his room at the approximate time of that death. Of course, the body might not be discovered immediately, or even for hours. And if it wasn't, his alibi would be worthless or at least seriously weakened.

But again, before he could feel any real sense of danger, a solution presented itself. Nothing was required but to leave his room immediately and proceed straight to the elevators. That gave him three witnesses instead of two. It proved—in the absence of contrary evidence—that he had gone downstairs within seconds after his second awakening.

Oh, it wasn't perfect, naturally. No alibi ever is. But it would take a finger to upset this one, and a finger was conspicuously absent. No one had seen him go to Dudley's room, no one had seen him leave. And so, necessarily, no one could say that he had been there.

Ed Gusick greeted him unctuously. Bugs responded with

his usual monosyllabic grunt, and got out of the car at the mezzanine. It was close to one o'clock now, and Rosalie Vara was absent; having her dinner in the kitchen, Bugs guessed. He walked down the mezz' to its far end, descended the staircase there to the lobby, and, turning to his left, entered the coffee shop.

It was a popular place, the one really good restaurant in town. And even at this hour, many of the tables and most of the counter stools were in use. Looking things over, automatically, Bugs glanced at a table in a far corner of the room, a table occupied by a taffy-haired young woman and a grinning, satanic-looking young man.

Bugs gulped, and his heart did a hop-skip. Ducking his head, he started for his usual stool at the end of the counter. But Lou Ford had already seen him.

"Hey, Bugs . . . McKenna!" He stood up and beckoned insistently. "Come on over!"

Bugs scowled and shook his head. Ford repeated his invitation at a shout. "Come on, fella! Don't be so skitterish. Got a friend here that wants to meet you!"

Bugs joined them; there was nothing else to do. Blushing, he mumbled an acknowledgement of Ford's jovial introduction to Amy Standish. Without raising his eyes, he gave his order to the waitress. He felt like his face was on fire. He felt like he was smothering. Practically all women affected him that way until he got to know them, but none had done so to the extent that Amy Standish did.

He heard an amused chuckle from Ford. Angrily, tossing the menu aside, he forced himself to look up.

Amy was smiling at him gently, her small round chin resting in the palm of her hand. "You mustn't mind him, Mr. McKenna"—she inclined her head toward the deputy. "He's just naturally ornery."

Bugs tried to smile back at her. He said he agreed with her in spades.

"Well, don't you mind, anyhow. We're friends now, so there's nothing to feel shy or awkward about."

"W-well . . . well, thanks," Bugs stammered. "I mean—"

"Heck, he ain't shy," Ford drawled. "He's just embarrassed. That's right, ain't it, Bugs? You're just embarrassed about that day you come up to the house and busted in without knockin'?"

"Shut up!" Bugs snarled. "I—if you don't shut up, I'll—"

"Yeah? What's the matter? I say somethin' wrong?"

Bugs glowered at him. Amy looked curiously from one man to another.

"What *is* the matter?" she said. "You may as well tell me, Lou, now that you've started to. I—No, Mr. McKenna. I'm sure this concerns me, and I want to hear what it is."

Ford grinned at Bugs. He spread his hands easily. "Why, it wasn't nothin', really. All I was going to say was that Bugs seen you in your birthday suit."

"Did he?" Amy looked at him steadily.

"Didn't have a stitch on that I could see," Ford said, "and I sure could have seen any, close as I was. Yes, sir, you went skittering out into the hallway, naked as a jaybird. Stood there puttin' on your underclothes while you was chewin' me out."

"Yes? Well, go on. You're surely not going to stop there, are you?"

Ford drawled that yes, he guessed he would stop there. "Probably ain't a real fittin' thing to talk about at table," he added, with unapologetic apology. "Kind of looks like I maybe already sort of spoiled Bugs's dinner."

Amy turned away from him. Seemingly, at least for the moment, he ceased to exist for her.

"Well?" she said. "Well, Mr. McKenna?" Her voice was quiet, too quiet. Her gaze too steady. "Well?" she repeated. "We—"

"Sounds like a deep subject," remarked Lou Ford. "Yes, sir, I'd say that was a plumb deep subject, and that's a fact."

Bugs suddenly shoved back his plate. He shoved back his chair and stood up. And Amy smiled at him mistily and also stood. She seemed to have been waiting for him to make the move. He took her arm, and they started for the door.

"Hey, wait a minute, now," Ford called after them. "Where y'all rushing off to?" But he didn't sound like he actually cared, only sardonically amused. And they continued on across the restaurant and out the door to the sidewalk.

Bugs had paid down on an old coupe out of his last salary

check, and it was parked a few doors down the street. He helped her into it and drove her home. Her house was a companion piece to Ford's—was, in fact, in the same block as his. And, as in his case, it had been her parents' home, and their parents' before them. They were both old family, Lou Ford and Amy Standish. The last survivors of two old families. Bugs considered that fact, taking another look at her in his mind's eye, and he decided that she must be older than he orginally thought. Around thirty maybe. Maybe as old as thirty-one.

He stopped the car. She smiled at him softly, spoke as though answering a question and making an explanation.

"I'll be thirty my next birthday," she said. "I've lived here all my life, and I've never gone with anyone but Lou. What would you do in my place?"

"What would I . . ."

"Considering my age and my background. Considering that there is a very limited number of eligible men in a place like this."

Bugs didn't see what she was driving at. Or, perhaps, he didn't care to admit that he saw it. He was pretty broad-minded, understand—by his own admission. And he'd fallen for this Amy Standish the moment he saw her. But falling for her, liking and wanting her, was one thing, and something else was something else. And he'd already had one chuck of second-hand goods.

"I guess I ought to be getting back to the job," he said uncomfortably. "Am I—can I see you again?"

"I don't know—Mac? Is it all right to call you that? I don't care for Bugs."

"I don't either, and Mac's fine. Well, how about it—Amy?"

"As I was saying, I don't know, Mac. I'm not sure that you should . . . No, it isn't that"—she anticipated him. "Lou has told me quite a bit about you, your past, and that isn't a factor at all. It's just that—that—"

"You think Lou might not like it?"

"I'm not sure. I can't tell you. But"—she smiled with sudden brightness, head tilted playfully to one side—"there's one thing I am sure of. Very sure of. In fact there are several things. I'm sure I like you a lot, and I'm sure you've got the kindest-looking eyes I've ever seen, and I'm sure"—she kissed him lightly on the mouth—"I've been wanting to do that for the last thirty minutes."

She laughed and scampered out the car. She turned her head back through the window. "And another thing. I'm sure you ask a great many questions on short acquaintance."

And then she was crying. The laughter had changed suddenly to tears.

Weeping, she fled up the walk to the house.

Bugs kicked open the door, called a question after her.

"Y-yes!" she stopped and whirled around. "Why shouldn't you see me? Why shouldn't anyone, everyone? Why—why—"

She started running again. Bugs let her go. After all, he was going to have this Dudley matter to deal with tonight. And he'd damned well better keep his mind on it until it was safely wrapped up. And, aside from that, well . . .

Well?

He cursed, cursing himself and Lou Ford with equal venom. Feeling frustrated, his mind churning with confusion, he drove back to the hotel.

Ford was loitering in front of the entrance, one boot heel hooked back against the bricks, one of his thin black cigars in the corner of his mouth. He slouched out to the curb as Bugs climbed out of his car.

"You're bein' paged," he announced. "Looks like you got a suicide on your hands."

"A suicide?" Bugs managed a satisfactory start. "Who was it? How did it happen?"

"Joyce Hanlon. Drank herself a cup of poison. Guess she heard about you bein' with Amy and it plumb broke her heart."

He nodded soberly, very long of face. Then, as Bugs gaped at him, he laughed and slapped the big man on the back. "Just jokin' with you, fella; doubt if they's anything on the market that would make a dent in Joyce."

"Very funny," Bugs snapped. "Look, has there actually been a suicide, or—"

"Oh, sure, there's been one all right. Sure looks like one anyway. Man name of—Well, let's see if you can guess.

Three guesses, and if you hit it right I'll give you a see-gar."

"Never mind, goddammit." Bugs started for the entrance. "Of all the—!"

"You mean you don't like see-gars?" Ford easily joined stride with him. "Well, seein' as you're so impatient-like, it was a fella named Dudley, Alec Dudley. You know him, I reckon?"

"Sure, I know him; he's the Hanlon's auditor. I don't mean I was well-acquainted with him, but—"

"Uh-huh. Then, you wouldn't have any idea why he'd kill himself? Don't know of any trouble he was in, or whether he was feelin' dee-spondent or anything like that?"

"No."

"Well, let's see what we can find out." Ford linked arms with him companionably. "Been waitin' for you to come back before I did any investigatin'. Me, I'm a great hand for observin' pro-to-col, as the sayin' is. Guess you might call it my greatest vice and my strongest virtue . . ."

They made the investigation together—if such a casual asking of questions and looking-about could be called an investigation. Then, an ambulance having removed Dudley's body, they stood once more at the entrance of the hotel.

Bugs didn't want to be there; not with Ford, at least. He wanted to be alone, to relax his taut nerves, to sort out his thoughts about Amy Standish. But the deputy held him as if by an invisible magnet. He didn't have anything to say. He simply rambled on and on, with his usual drawling, rube-ish chit-chat, until Bugs was on the point of crawling out of his own skin.

And then Ford broke off suddenly, staring at Bugs out of shrewd, narrowly amused eyes. "Ain't you got some work to do?" he inquired, his voice soft-hard. "Hadn't you maybe ought to be gettin' at it?"

Bugs said he had. He added curtly that he couldn't very well work while he was standing around listening to a lot of goddamned nonsense.

Ford nodded equably. He took the cigar from his mouth, and examined the tip. And then, swiftly, he looked up, his gaze striking into Bugs's face like a blow.

"Why listen to it, then?" he said. "Why not just say good-night or go to hell, and turn around and walk off? You're all paid up with the law. You got a clean conscience—I reckon. So what's the answer? What are you afraid of? Why put up with me a minute more than you care to?"

Bugs looked down at the walk, not answering him. He couldn't. He couldn't put his feelings into words, nor, naturally, would he have dared to if he could have. He was guilty, technically guilty of at least manslaughter. There was a growing impression in his mind that he had been given his job for a sinister purpose, and that tacitly he had agreed to that purpose. So he could be held by Ford, forced to bend to him. And Ford knew it, and he was making him admit it.

The silence lasted for seeming hours. Then Ford cleared his throat, and his tone was casual again.

"Looks like you made quite a hit with Amy. Can't say when I've seen her quite so taken with a fella. How'd you like her anyway?"

"I liked her fine," Bugs said gruffly. "A lot more than I should, I guess."

"Yeah?"

"I mean, well, I'm just getting a start here. Never really had anything in my life, and don't know that I ever will have. And if she's your fiancee . . ."

"Mmm? Well, yeah, I believe I did say that, didn't I? But that's kind of a loose expression out this a-way. Gal and a fella goes steady for years, it's just kind of taken for granted that they're engaged. Don't really have to do nothin' or say nothin' about it themselves."

"Well," said Bugs. "I—uh—see."

"Had an idea you didn't like the way I talked to her tonight. Kind of got the impression you didn't like it a-tall."

"I didn't! I thought it was a goddamned lousy thing to do!"

"Yeah? Uh-huh?"

"What do you mean, 'yeah, uh-huh'?"

"I mean, you got some right not to like it? I mean, just what the hell is she to you for you to like or dislike it? Sure, you ain't got nothing, but you're still young and you're a pretty fair figure of a man, and Amy ain't the kind to count the money in your pocket. She was pretty taken with you; that's all that counts with her. And you seemed to reciprocate the feeling. And remember, I ain't standin' in your way. Got too much pride to use my job in a personal matter, even if I did want to . . . So let's have your answer. Just what the hell is she to you? Or maybe I should say, what'd you like to have her be to you?"

"Hell." Bugs squirmed. "What's this all about, anyway? I'm busy, and I hardly know the girl and—"

"You can be unbusy a minute longer. And maybe you know her too well. You feel like you know her too well, and you don't like what you know."

"For God's sake, Ford! I told you that—"

"Why don't you say it? Spit it out. Say that she might be all right for you to play around with, but she ain't good enough for anything more."

So all right, Bugs thought savagely. *I do feel that way, kind of. And how can you blame me for that?*

He didn't say anything, however.

Although he might as well have.

Ford stared at him, lip curling, his face a mask of profane wonderment. "Well, I," he said, incredulously, "I will be a son-of-a-bitch! Never let no one call me that in my life, but I'll say it myself. I will be a dirty double-donged son-of-a-bitch! . . . A jailbird like you. A stupid, stubborn jerk that never did a damned thing right in his life, that's fouled up everything, and you think . . ."

He turned slowly and walked away.

Scowling defensively, Bugs re-entered the hotel. So maybe he had botched up his whole life. Or, rather, since it wasn't his fault, it had been botched up for him. That was why he had to be extra careful now. Because he wasn't so young any more, and just about one more wrong move would foul him up for good.

And just where—and this was what completely bewildered Bugs—where did Ford get off at lecturing another guy about Amy? He was no good, a crook and a grafter. She'd been a sweet clean girl, and he'd made her into something not so sweet and clean. And then, the low-down louse, he kidded her about it in front of a stranger! He was that kind of guy, he did that to her. And yet he had the gall to bawl out the aforesaid stranger for his entirely natural concern with what had happened before he came along!

Hell, Bugs thought, *I didn't say I held it against her, did I? Hell, she's still going with him, isn't she? Hell, I just met her, didn't I? Hell . . .*

Hell, hell, hell!

Bugs stood in a corner of the vaulted lobby, smoking a cigarette in short angry puffs. Noting absently that Rosalie Vara had returned from her dinner—or wherever she had been—and was once again at work on the mezz'.

She saw him looking at her and flirted a hand at him. He grinned back weakly, and sauntered toward the elevators.

Well, nuts, he thought. He was getting all up in the air over nothing. Getting the cart a mile in front of the horse. This was a hell of a time to be thinking about Amy Standish, her or any other woman. To be thinking about anything except hanging onto his job, and staying out of trouble. And he wouldn't have been if Ford hadn't hailed him there in the coffee shop, and acted like the double-distilled son-of-a-bitch which he admitted being.

Well. Well, maybe it was all for the best. Maybe Ford had done him a favor. He hadn't been afraid, exactly, but naturally he'd been pretty shaken up over what had happened to Dudley. And then Ford had latched onto him, diverting his mind from Dudley until it could accept his death without shock. Until he was prepared to face up to the death in front of Ford with no telltale nervousness.

Yeah, everything had worked out for the best. The means hadn't been exactly pleasant, maybe, but the result had been perfect. Because he was safe, now. He'd been in a mess that might have meant curtains for him, but now he was safe.

He wondered why he felt so lousy.

He wondered why, meaning as well as he did, he was always getting into messes.

Bugs was working as a guard in an aircraft plant
. . . when World War II broke out. Since the beginning
of his working career, he had almost always landed in jobs
as a night watchman or a guard or something of the kind.
He wasn't trained for a well-paying position—the kind a
man might be proud to hold. And having a little authority,
even at relatively low pay, helped to buck up his ego.

This particular job was somewhat better than average,
and Bugs did his best to hold onto it. He did everything he
was supposed to, nothing that he shouldn't; sticking to the
rule book right to the letter. And his best wasn't good
enough.

The chief engineer's wife showed up at the plant one day.
She had a pass, as was required, but she also had a sealed
package. And Bugs, over her vehement protests, insisted
on opening it. It contained a box of sanitary napkins.

She departed the plant in tears. About thirty minutes
later—just as quickly as she could reach her husband by telephone and he could get in touch with the plant
superintendent—Bugs departed with his final paycheck.

The loss of the job lost him his draft deferment. Bugs
went into the Army where he shortly found himself an MP.
He was patrolling the airplane hangars one evening when
he discovered a man in a Russian officer's uniform prowling amongst the planes. Accosted by Bugs, the man complimented him on his alertness, and displayed the credentials
of an American general.

Well. As Bugs admitted at his court-martial, he recognized the credentials as genuine; he had even recognized
the general. Still, the masquerade had been a damned stupid thing, a violation of regulations in itself. And he, Bugs,
had been entirely within his rights in insisting that the general march ahead of him to a guard post where an officer
could dispose of his case. The general had refused, pro-
fanely and violently. He had started to walk away from
Bugs. Bugs told him to halt. When he kept on going, Bugs
shot him in the hip.

The shooting cost him two years in the Army stockade.

He was also sentenced to a dishonorable discharge, but a higher court toned that down to a discharge under honorable conditions, also remitting six months of his previously forfeited pay.

He was in San Diego, looking around and resting on the money when he met his wife-to-be.

It happened one Sunday, at the city's justly famous zoo. Bugs was standing in front of the monkey cages, one of the crowd of people tossing peanuts through the bars and watching the animals' antics. He was standing there gawking and grinning, and thinking he looked pretty nice in his new suit of clothes, when a monkey reached behind him suddenly, came up with a brimming handful of ordure, and flung it all over him.

Talk about messes. He looked like he'd just crawled through a sewer. And everyone was laughing at him, really knocking themselves out. And he didn't know what the hell he was going to do; how he could get across town ten miles to his room where he could wash up and change clothes.

Then a hand touched his arm, closed over it gently, and he looked down into a face that wasn't laughing, but only tender and sympathetic. And he realized later that a dame didn't get a pan on her like that in less than forty years. But at the time, she looked like an angel to him.

She had a little apartment nearby. He was more than welcome to come there and get himself in order. Gratefully, he accepted the invitation.

He bathed and scrubbed himself, while she worked over his clothes in the kitchen. Then, with a sheet pulled around him, he sat down on the bed to wait for the return of the garments. She came in with them, finally, dressed in a robe. She started to hand them to him, and somehow accidentally-on-purpose her robe fell open. And apparently she'd had some laundry to do of her own, because she sure as hell wasn't wearing any.

Naturally, she was thoroughly mortified. As she put it, she felt just like sinking through the floor. By the way of compromise, she sank down on the bed instead, where, needless to say, her nudity was promptly covered with more of the same.

She wept bitterly afterwards. Bugs almost made with the tears himself. It was her first experience with a man—possibly excepting the members of the Pacific Fleet and the local Marine contingent—and he was dismayed at having despoiled her.

They were married in Arizona the next day. It was the very least he could do—to make her an honorable woman.

Two weeks later, when he came down with practically every disease in the venereal category, he was still too unawakened to connect her with them, and was completely satisfied with her theory as to how they had been contracted.

Fortunately, for himself, at least, he had just taken a job where a physical examination was necessary. And with the ancientest of medical jokes, the doctor rid him of his childish naivete.

"A toilet stool, eh?" he said. "Do you sleep with a toilet stool?"

"Of course, I don't," Bugs frowned. "I sleep with my wife."

"No one else? Don't do any playing around? Well, then," said the doctor. "Well, then, young man?" And he spread his hands significantly.

Bugs almost killed her. Except for the arrival of the police, he might have been beating on her yet.

Arrested and held for trial, he would give no reason for the assault. He had too much pride; he was too ashamed of being taken for a sucker.

He was sentenced to six months in the county jail, plus permanent banishment from the state. Released, he started drifting, arriving eventually in Texas.

In the mushrooming towns-become-cities, municipal employees were at a premium—particularly if they were young and able-bodied and had anything at all in the way of police experience. Bugs fitted those specifications. He also was an honorably discharged veteran. True, he had a bad record, but in those hectic days a man might work a very long time before his record caught up with him, if it ever did.

Bugs became a city police patrolman. After three months, during which there was an almost one hundred per cent turnover in the department's personnel, he was promoted to plain clothes. It was in that job that he landed in his biggest and worst scrape.

One of the other dicks was a wild-eyed, constantly grinning boob with a penchant for practical jokes. He didn't bother the other guys much, and so was fairly well-liked by them. But to Bugs, who had been fiendishly singled out as a born butt, he was nothing less than maddening.

He was going off watch one evening when the guy lurched through the door of the locker-room. He was more wild-eyed than usual; drunk apparently. Yanking out his gun, he announced that he had taken as much off of Bugs as he intended to, and that now he was going to kill him.

Murmuring protests, pulling long faces, the other dicks got out of the way. Among them was one, who, only a moment before, had asked to take a look at Bugs's gun, with a view of making a swap.

Bugs spoke to him out of the corner of his mouth; begged him for God's sake to return the weapon. The man didn't seem to hear him. Sweating, he whispered a plea for someone to do something—to step in and stop this character. No one seemed to hear that entreaty either. Or, ostensibly, they were too shocked or frightened to heed it.

Bugs let out a roar of fear. Leaping sideways suddenly, he snatched back his borrowed gun, whirled and fired. He emptied the chamber. And at that distance, of course, he couldn't miss.

The dick was dead before he hit the floor. To state what is probably obvious, he had only been playing another of his practical jokes, and the other dicks had all been in on it.

It had been a crazy trick to pull. In fact, as was established at the autopsy, the guy *was* crazy. His erratic behavior was due to a tumor of the brain, which, in another year or less, would certainly have killed him. So Bugs couldn't really be blamed for what he had done. And with a different attitude on his part, the matter might have ended with a departmental investigation.

Unfortunately . . .

Well, you can probably guess what his attitude was; it was anything but proper to a situation where a man's life had been lost.

He was goddamned glad he'd killed the son-of-a-bitch, he said. He should have done it long before. Given the opportunity, he'd do the same thing all over again.

He surlily repeated those statements at the inevitable trial. Those and others that were equally damning. He shouted them as he was hauled out of the courtroom, the recipient of the stiffest jolt that the law could give him. And now, tossing in his sleep . . .

I'm glad, he told himself. *I've done nothing to be sorry about. He—they—she's got no one to blame but herself. I've got principles, by God, and no one's ever made me change 'em. And she— Christ, I wish I didn't have. I wish—*

He lurched and sat up in bed. It was eleven o'clock in the morning, a few minutes after eleven, and the phone was ringing.

He picked it up, spoke with drowsy grumpiness. "Yeah? 'S'McKenna."

"This is Mike Hanlon, Bugs. Mr. Hanlon. I'd like to see you."

"See me?" Bugs's throat tightened unconsciously. "Uh, now, you mean?"

"Now," said Hanlon. And hung up the receiver.

It was the second time, since the date of his employment, that Bugs had talked with Hanlon. The first occasion had been about ten days after he came to the hotel, when, at the old man's request—or order—he had taken him along on his nightly tour of the building.

Hanlon had had to be in his wheelchair, of course, and in place of the stairs they had moved from floor to floor in one of the out-of-use elevators. The cars were very simple to operate, Bugs learned. Hanlon had taught him all there was to know about it in a few minutes, also showing him how to open the elevator door from the outside.

Thinking back on that evening, several incidents which had had no meaning for him at the time began to acquire significance.

Bugs had unlocked the car—you did it by inserting a short rod through two holes in the door and bearing downward. He had started to wheel Hanlon into its darkened interior, and the old man had gripped the wheels of his chair, holding it immobile. If Bugs didn't mind, he said wryly, he'd like the car's lights turned on before entering it.

Bugs turned them on. Studying him shrewdly, Hanlon had explained the reason for his request.

"Like to make sure the car's actually there, y'know. Can't really tell without the lights on. Might not be anything but the empty shaft."

"But why wouldn't it be there?" Bugs looked at him blankly. "If I left it with the door closed—"

"Isn't exactly hard to open, is it? Do it with practically anything strong enough to bear a little weight. Yeah"—Hanlon nodded slowly—"things like that have happened. A bellboy gets impatient and takes a floored car. Or a maintenance engineer thinks it's been stalled, and takes it for a test trip. Or maybe it's just a fluke; the thing slips on its cables. That's happened, too, with cars that get a lot of heavy service. Anyway," he concluded, "I don't enter any elevators unless I'm sure there's one to enter."

He had said, rather shyly, that there was a swell view from the roof, so Bugs had taken him up there. He had wheeled him up close to the parapet, and together, fourteen stories up, they had looked out over the twinkling, thundering, garishly-lit forest of derricks. The smell of crude oil was in the air; the smell of natural gas, fresh from its mile-deep storehouses; the smell of drilling mud, and salt water and sulphur.

Hanlon sniffed the breeze hungrily. Wasn't that something? he asked. Wasn't that really something? Bugs said it smelled a lot like rotten eggs to him. The old man stiffened but ignored the comment.

"That's death out there, Bugs. All over out there. All dressed up, and with his pockets full of dollar bills . . . It's the most dangerous business in the world, did you know that? Coal-mining, construction—they aren't in it with the oil fields. Well, it's not so bad now that the big companies have moved in, but the kind of operation I used to run, that the average wildcatter runs—God Almighty! Insurance costs you practically as much as your payroll . . . Yep, it's death everywhere you turn, and Bugs, it never bothered me much. Not out there. I met the old boy day after day, and I didn't like him naturally. But I wasn't worried about him, I wasn't afraid of him. Out there . . ."

A gust of wind whipped across the roof. It snatched the robe from the old man's knees, and Bugs grabbed at it, his arm striking against and rocking the chair. Instantly, he found himself looking down the barrel of a gun which the robe had concealed.

"Hey!" he grunted, more surprised than alarmed. "What are you doing with that?"

Hanlon hesitated; laughed apologetically. "You know, I'd forgot I had the thing with me? I was cleaning it today, and I must have shoved it in my pocket afterward. Didn't discover it until now, just as that robe blew off, and when I made a grab for the robe . . ."

He left the sentence unfinished. Bugs held out his hand. "Mind if I take a look at it?"

"Why?"—sharply. "Why do you want to look at it?"

Bugs was immediately haughty. "If you put it that way, I don't want to. Forget I asked you."

Hanlon handed it to him, insisted that he look at it. But the gun was kind of a pet with him, apparently, for he kept his eyes on it every second. Bugs could understand his attitude—what he thought was his attitude. He liked a good gun himself. Somewhat mollified, he examined it and started to hand it back.

"Carry it for me, Bugs. Keep it until we get back to the suite . . ."

"That's all right," Bugs said, misunderstanding. "I just wanted to look at it."

"No, I'd like to have you do it. It's kind of awkward for me in this chair."

Bugs carried it back to the suite for him. There Hanlon asked him to prepare a dose of his medicine. "It's in the cabinet above the sink. The round bottle with the blue and white label. I take three drops in a half-glass of water."

Bugs entered the bathroom. He drew exactly one-half glass of water, and cautiously dripped exactly three drops of the fluid into it. He turned to leave, and there was

Hanlon, his chair wheeled up into the doorway.

"Thought I'd have you give me a drink of cold water first," he explained. "Mouth seems to have got a little dry up there on the roof."

Bugs gave it to him, gave him the medicine. He said then that he guessed he'd better be shoving off unless Hanlon wanted something else.

"Nothing, thanks. And Bugs"—he grinned in an odd way—"thanks very much for the excursion. I can't tell you how much good it's done me."

"Glad to do it," Bugs said gruffly. "Any time you'd like to go again, just holler."

"We-ell . . . I wouldn't feel right about asking you, telling you to do it. It's a lot of extra work for you, and you're not paid to play nursemaid."

"Hell, it's no trouble. I really don't mind at all, Mr. Hanlon," Bugs insisted.

"Well, I'll leave it up to you, anyway." Hanlon said. "I'm usually up pretty late. Any time you feel like you'd like to have a little company, or there's something you'd like to talk to me about, why, just stop by. Don't need to call beforehand. Just knock on the door, and I'll be rarin' to go."

Bugs was touched by the old man's eagerness. Moreover, he sensed Hanlon's very genuine liking for him, and, appearances to the contrary, he hungered for liking. So he said they'd be seeing a lot of each other; he'd be dropping by soon and often. And he really meant to. And then he had got to mulling over the implications of the situation—implications which would never have occurred to anyone but him—and he had never dropped by. Nor did he intend to, unless so ordered.

It just wouldn't do, you see. Hanlon would misunderstand. Hanlon would think he was sucking up to him, that he was the kind of guy who went around brown-nosing the boss. If he was ordered to wheel him around, okay. He *did* want to keep his job, so he'd follow orders to the letter. But even then he wouldn't knock himself out being pleasant, as (in his own mind) he had done before. He'd make it clear that this wasn't his job, that he wasn't a *nursemaid*—to use a term which the old man had tactlessly used himself.

. . . He knocked on the parlor of Hanlon's suite. Receiving no answer, he unlocked the door with his emergency key—a key used in opening doors locked from the inside—and went in.

Hanlon was on the terrace, his chair drawn up to an umbrella-shaded table. He heard Bugs's entrance, and gestured a greeting to him. And Bugs crossed the room and went out through the French doors.

"Coffee?" The old man motioned to a chair, and poured from a silver pot. "Sorry if I got you out of bed, Bugs."

"That's all right," Bugs said, not too graciously. "What's on your mind, Mr. Hanlon?"

"Westbrook." Hanlon took out a cigarette, looked at Bugs over the tip. "I tried to get in touch with him early this morning. When I couldn't, I had his room checked. It hadn't been slept in. He's nowhere in the hotel. I wonder if you know where he could have gone to?"

"Me?" Bugs set down his cup, and it rattled slightly against the saucer. "How would I know?"

"I just asked . . . give me a light, will you?"

Bugs held a match for him. Hanlon gripped his hand and steadied it, looking into his eyes.

"Did you talk to him yesterday, Bugs? Or last night, I should say?"

"No."

"Sure about that? One of the maids, that pretty little Vara gal, saw him last night on your floor. According to the telephone operator, you were still in your room at the time. I don't know of any reason why he would have been up there except to see you."

A bead of sweat rolled down Bugs's forehead. A weak, silly laugh welled out of his throat.

"Oh, well, yeah," he laughed again. "Ollie did stop by to see me for a few minutes. But it was after midnight, y'know; think it was, anyhow. It was this morning, not last night. When you asked me if I'd seen him last night, why—why—"

"Never mind." Hanlon grimaced distastefully. "What did he want to see you about?"

"Nothing much. I—Look, Mr. Hanlon." Bugs had a seeming inspiration. "I didn't want to tell you about his coming to see me, because he'd been drinking quite a bit. I thought if you found out he was wandering around—"

"I need you to tell me that Ollie drinks? You think I didn't know it? Now, *you* look!" Hanlon crashed his fist down on the table. "I wasn't born yesterday or even the day before. I've been around, get me? I'm not stupid, get me? I'm supposed to be smart, get me, and I damned well am. And if you're half-way smart, you'll start talking!"

He leaned back in his chair, shakily. After a moment, he said. "All right, I'm waiting."

Bugs nodded. "All right. I didn't want to tell you about it because . . . well, you'll see why. Ollie did a quarterly audit of the books last night. He discovered a big shortage—better than five thousand dollars. He couldn't prove it, but he was sure that Dudley had knocked down the money. . . ."

"That's right," Hanlon said, as though he were following a recitation with the text. "I knew it was something like that. I warned Ollie against the bastard. I hate to speak ill of the dead, but I told Ollie at the time that if there ever was a sneak and a sharper—Excuse me, Bugs. You were saying!"

"Well, that's about it. He was worried to death. He figured this place was his last chance, if he lost out here he'd never get another job, and he was sure you'd fire him."

"And he didn't miss it either! When you warn and warn a man about something, and he still goes right ahead and . . . well," Hanlon sighed grudgingly, "I guess I'd probably give him another chance. Shouldn't but I would. He's a mighty good little man, and I can't really fault him for being loyal to his friends."

Bugs was calming down a little. He said it was nice of Hanlon to feel that way.

"Just practical, Bugs. Just practical." The old man leaned forward confidentially. "Do you suppose he will show up again? In a few days, you know, as soon as he snaps out of his drunk?"

"Well, sure. Why not?"

"You can't think of any reason why not? Don't try to cover up, Bugs, for him or me. It just wouldn't wash. I'd hate it if it's like it could be—like I was afraid it might be. It would cause a hell of a scandal, get us into a whopping lawsuit if Dudley had anything as close as a fourth cousin. But I still couldn't go for a cover-up. So if Ollie had anything to do with what happened to Dudley—"

"He didn't," Bugs said steadily. "He knew it wouldn't do him any good to see Dudley." He elaborated briefly, explaining the matter as Westbrook had explained it to him. Hanlon seemed something less than satisfied.

"We-ell, I'll buy that part. Ollie's a practical guy, drunk or sober, and he wouldn't have talked to Dudley when he knew it wouldn't make him anything. Still, he is missing. And five thousand dollars is missing. And Dudley is dead."

"Dudley could have spent the money," Bugs shrugged. "He could have had it cached somewhere. And as low as Ollie was feeling . . ."

"Yes, I can see that, too. He can't face the music, so he just goes off on a bat. He's done the same thing in other places. But this suicide—" Hanlon lingered over the word. "As a cop, Bugs, doesn't that jar the hell out of you? Dudley's stolen the money. He's gotten away with it; he can't be touched. That being the case, why—"

"It beats me." Bugs shook his head soberly. "Probably there was some trouble in his past. Something that finally caught up with him."

"Well, yes. That could be, of course. And, of course, if a suicide behaved logically he wouldn't be a suicide. Yes, that figures. It's not so unreasonable when you look on it that way. You've taken a great load off my mind, Bugs."

Bugs murmured modestly. He held another match for Hanlon's cigarette.

"But I'm still left with one question"—the old man blew out the flame. "Rather, I'm left without the answer to one question. I wonder if you'd like to supply it."

Bugs looked blank. Or tried to. But he knew what Hanlon meant; it was the question he'd been dreading . . . Why had Westbrook visited him the night before? Just to babble? Just to explain his predicament, to weep on a friendly shoulder? Or for another and very practical reason?

That was the question troubling Hanlon, Bugs knew. Essentially the only question. The one he'd been leading up to right from the beginning. And he knew something else: that Hanlon didn't really give a whoop about Dudley, *per se*. That he was only mildly worried, if at all, about the possibility of a scandal or a lawsuit. He was interested in Dudley's death, only in so far as it might be the forerunner of his own. For if Bugs had killed Dudley, if he would kill for money . . .

And Bugs couldn't admit what he knew. He couldn't confess to his growing conviction—or suspicions—that he had been hired for the purpose of murdering Hanlon. Obviously, he couldn't. The admission that he entertained such suspicions, while continuing to remain on the job, would be damning in itself.

"I don't know what you're talking about," Bugs said. "Maybe you'd better tell me."

"I'll tell you one thing, Bugs. I'm not doing Ford any favors, and I'm not interested in playing cops and robbers . . . or killers. Anything you say will be strictly between us. So if it was an accident—or even something a little more than that. If you were just trying to do Ollie a favor, and you lost your temper or—"

"I don't know what you're talking about," Bugs repeated. "But I sure don't like the way it sounds. Now, either stop beating around the bush, or throw your stick away. Otherwise, I'm walking out of here, and if I do I'll keep right on going!"

That did it; the return to his normal surliness. Hanlon's eyes searched his face, the haunted look in them giving way to relief.

"Forget it, Bugs," he said. "It's nothing important. Just a foolish idea I had for a moment."

"Well . . ."

"Forget it. And thanks very much for stopping by."

Bugs started to leave. At the doors to the terrace, he paused and turned around. He didn't know why he did it at the moment. He didn't know why he said what he did. It was something instinctive, a long step forward—or downward—taken into the darkness of the future.

"I was just thinking," he said. "I promised I'd pick you up some night and we'd do the rounds together . . ."

"Yes? Oh, yes, I guess you did," said Hanlon. "Well, I didn't really expect you to bother about it."

"No bother. Would you—I don't suppose you'd still like to go, would you?"

Hanlon hesitated for the merest fraction of a second. He

seemed to waver a little, to melt and lose form like candy over a hot flame. Then, as though plunged suddenly into cold water, he was himself again. Reassembled into a harder, steadier self than he had been that split second before.

"Yes," he said, "I'd still like to go. Why not, Bugs?"

"I'll do it then," Bugs said. "I'll stop by . . . some night."

He returned to his room, and went back to bed. Lying there wakefully, too tired to sleep, rested just sufficiently to keep him from resting more, he struggled with a question. *Why did I invite him, anyway? I didn't have to. He didn't expect me to. So, why? Why?*

The answer finally came to him. Aided by weariness, it weeded its way through the many mental blocks he had set up. Burst forth into his consciousness.

And, yes, you know it. It scared hell out of him.

It was three days after Dudley's death that Bugs received the letter. A blackmail letter demanding the five thousand dollars which he had supposedly murdered Dudley to obtain. The writer left no doubt about the fact that he, or rather she—it just about had to be a she—meant business. She made it clear that she had the goods on him—and she did have in a hideously false but irrefutable way—and that, failing to get the five thousand, she would turn the matter over to Lou Ford.

So Bugs was back again in his natural habitat: that vulgarly named creek which he always seemed to wind up in. And this time he was not only without a paddle but also a boat.

Because, naturally, he didn't have and couldn't get the five thousand which he had to have, or else. He couldn't get five hundred. He couldn't have scraped up fifty without seriously straining himself.

That left him with only one alternative. To find out who the blackmailer was. To find her and give her something in place of the five thousand. This presented something of a problem, of course. But he had a good strong lead on the dame, a pretty good idea of who she was—he thought. So it boiled down to a matter of leading her on, concealing his suspicions, and then—

But that was then. All that began on the third day after Dudley's death.

Taking things as they came, the events following his interview with Mike Hanlon:

. . . Bugs had a hard time getting to sleep. In fact, it was almost three in the afternoon before he finally did doze off. Then, around six, he was awakened by a soft but persistent rapping. And his several who-is-its and what-is-its being ignored, he yanked on his trousers and went to the door.

It was Joyce Hanlon, dressed in her usual uniform of flank-fitting skirt and overstuffed sweater. She smiled at him brightly, and Bugs tried to smile back at her. The best he could manage was a fearsome baring of teeth.

"Hi, Bugs," she said. "Were you asleep?"

"Asleep? Oh, no, nothing like that," he laughed hoarsely. "No, I never sleep in the daytime. I do that at night when I'm walking around the hotel."

"Oh . . . Well, I hope I didn't wake you up."

Bugs let out an angry moan. He tried to control himself, to smirk politely, to say it was all right and that it didn't matter a bit. But—but—

She *hoped* she hadn't waked him up! Goddammit, he'd just got through telling her that he was asleep, and then she *hoped* she hadn't waked him up!

How goddamned stupid could you get, anyway? And what did she want, anyway?

The questions growled and snarled through his mind. They rushed out of his mouth before he could stop them.

Her eyes widened, and she took a startled backward step. *"Well!"* she said. "I can't say that I appreciate—"

"Who gives a damn? I just got to sleep, for Christ's sake, and then you—I—all right, I'm sorry. I didn't mean to blow my top, but—"

"Now, that's better," she said primly. "Well, aren't you going to invite me in?"

"Hell, I guess so. I mean, certainly, glad to have you. I—Aah, to hell with it. Come in or stay out, whatever you damned please."

She marched past him, mouth quirked, cheeks flushed. She sat down on the bed gingerly, and Bugs closed the door with a bang, slouched down in a chair in front of her.

She crossed her legs, brushed at a tiny crease in her skirt. Bugs plucked at an imaginary hangnail. They looked up, and their eyes met. They looked quickly down again, and then slowly up again.

And suddenly she exploded into laughter, flung herself backward on the bed, her heels drumming against its sides, her entire body quivering and quaking with amusement.

"Oh, Bugs—*ha*, *ha*—the way you looked, like some old bear just out of its cave! And when I asked you if you'd been asleep—*ha*, *ha*, *ha*—when I asked you—*oooh-whoops*, *ha*, *ha*, *ha*, *ha* . . ."

Bugs grinned, chuckled self-consciously, tried to keep his eyes off those long, luciously fleshed legs. He said he guessed he had acted like the king of the grouches, and that she shouldn't let it bother her.

"Now, don't apologize. I'm glad. I feel like I'm finally getting acquainted with you, and I was beginning to think I never would . . . Come here."

"Uh—where? What for?" Bugs said.

"*Here*, silly!" She held up her arms, wiggled her fingers at him. "Here to mama. And what do you think, what for?"

So that was how it came about. That was how Bugs wound up in the hay with Joyce Hanlon, the wife of his employer. By talking ugly, telling her to go jump, to go to hell and like it or lump it. That broke the ice between them, advanced their relationship to a point which might ordinarily have taken months to achieve.

But it was a hay-roll only in the literal sense. Just a petting spree, with plenty of kissing and clinching, and probing and pinching, but without the usual climax. And it was no fault of Bugs's that the climax was missing.

He might be strait-laced, prudish, but a man changes under enough stress. Also, he couldn't feel that he was depriving or injuring Hanlon; the old man would be disappointed in him, perhaps, but he wouldn't care about her. So, such credit as was due for their continence, was due to Joyce. It was she who held off, holding him just far enough, letting him go just far enough, to keep a firm grip on him.

That, she said, was a bedtime story. *That* wasn't nice. *That* was something she really couldn't bring herself to do—yet.

"But why not, dammit! If you didn't intend to—"

"Because, that's why. Now, be a sweet darling, hmm? Give Joyce one of those real pretty smiles."

"Horseshit!"

"With sugar on it? Hmm? Hmm? Come on, now, grouchy. Let's see you smile."

She tickled him in the ribs. Bugs squirmed, grinned unwillingly.

"Now, that's better . . . What did Mike want with you this morning, honey? What did he talk to you about?"

"Nothing. How do you know he talked to me at all?"

"Now, Bugs. I'm a very bright little girl, and the wife of the owner finds out lots of things."

"Then, find out what he talked to me about . . . Well, hell," Bugs said, "it wasn't anything much. Just wanted a report on the suicide. Why I thought Dudley had done it, and so on."

"Yes?"

"Well, he was short in his books I know. At least, Westbrook said he was. Incidentally, I suppose you've heard that Westbrook has—"

"Yes, yes," Joyce cut in. "Forget Westbrook. All I'm interested in is Dudley."

"Why? You and him pally, were you?"

"Now, silly. I hardly knew him to speak to. I doubt if I'd ever passed a half-a-dozen words with him. Why—"

"Whoa, whoa up, now"—Bugs drew his head back to look at her. "I just asked you a question. It's not a federal case."

"Well, I didn't know Dudley at all! He was just another one of the employees, as far as I was concerned. I only asked about him because of you."

"Yeah?"

"Yes! Now, stop it, Bugs! This is serious. Did Mike—did he blame you? I mean—well, you know. Do you think he, uh, held it against you for any reason? That he, uh, trusted you any the less because of it?"

Bugs was getting tired. Perhaps because of his increasing

awareness that that was all he was going to get. He studied her covertly, noting the tiny wrinkles around her eyes, a thin furrow of powder on her neck—a dozen distasteful things which the excitement of sex play had blinded him to. Self-disgust rose in his throat. He felt ashamed dirty, filthy. He told himself—and he meant it—that he wouldn't take her now if she was served up on a platter.

God, what had he been thinking about, anyway? What kind of a guy was he getting to be? He knew what she was angling for, and here he'd gone right ahead and jumped at the bait.

"No, Joyce," he said. "No, he does not trust me any less, Joyce. Not one damned bit. And do you know why he doesn't, Joyce? Because he knows damned well he doesn't have any reason to. And, Joyce, he never will have!"

He nodded his head firmly. Joyce gave him a playful pat on the cheek, spoke with forced lightness.

"Now, isn't that nice? That's real nice, isn't it?"

"Yes," said Bugs. "I think it's very nice."

"It's too bad that he isn't a younger man. That he's sick and old. He might do a great deal for you. You're still young, and—What's the matter, honey?" Her eyes shifted nervously. "Why are you looking at me like that?"

"I was just thinking," Bugs said. "You know I used to play a lot of football? Pretty good at the game at one time."

"Football? But what—"

"It isn't worth getting up for, so I was wondering. Whether I could give you a good hard kick in the ass from a prone position."

"*Wh-aat!*" She let out a gasp, sat up angrily. "Well, of all—"

Bugs hand slid under her buttocks. He boosted, viciously, and she soared from the bed, came down on her feet on the floor.

"Now, beat it," he said. "Clear out before I bounce you out."

She sputtered furiously. Her eyes raged for a moment; there was something close to murder in them. And then she laughed. Laughing down his threats. Leaving him frustrated and disarmed.

She wouldn't get angry with him. She was not the kind to get angry where it would cost her. And after her first brief flash of temper, she had felt no anger. The rough stuff—she'd been weaned on it. She'd known plenty of guys who substituted a kick in the slats for a kiss, and more than once she had found herself thinking of them fondly. They weren't so bad, some of those fellows. At least, a girl never got bored around them.

So as Bugs grumbled and cursed futilely, she sat down on the bed, again; rumpled his hair, patted and poked him with caressing tenderness.

"Now, just stop it, you old bear . . . big overgrown brute. I'll come back tonight after you've rested, and—"

"You'd by-God better not come back tonight!"

"Well, soon then. Whatever you say. We'll have a nice, sweet talk real soon, and maybe . . ."

"Get out of here! . . ."

"Okay, Mama knows he's tired, so she'll just tuck him in real good, and—"

"Mama? *Mama!*" Bugs's voice cracked with outrage. "Jesus Christ, what kind of a woman are you, anyway? How the hell can—"

"Now, now. Just hold your legs out like a good boy."

She gripped the cuffs of his trousers, pulled them off expertly. Draping them over a chair, she tucked the bed-clothes up under his chin and planted a lingering kiss upon his mouth.

"Now," she said, gathering up her purse. "Now, you'll sleep *good!* . . ."

It was probably the misstatement of the century. Despite two cold showers and four aspirins, he didn't sleep at all. And it did no damned good at all to tell himself that he was eight kinds of a heel, and that he ought to be ashamed.

He was *ashamed*. He was also frightened—plenty. But it didn't change anything.

He was so far gone that when Rosalie Vara came to do his room, he made occasion to brush against her.

She stood perfectly motionless for a moment, still bent over from the bedspread. Then, gently but firmly, her rounded hips returned the pressure of his body.

Bugs got out of the room fast.

By morning, he was approximately his old self again. He had wallowed in worry and reproach, shrived his shamed soul with the acid of disgust; and then finally he had emerged, shaky, a little frayed around the edges. But also spotless—practically—and filled with firm resolve.

Dammit, every man had an occasional weak moment. Every man played the jerk at least once. That didn't mean, however, that he was a weak man, or that he would continue to be a jerk. On the contrary, he was better off for having got the nonsense out of his system.

Bugs was all right now, he told himself. He was back on the ball again, and he intended to stay there. There'd be no more of this hank-panky. Not only that, but he'd steer clear of any and all situations which might lead to such.

He hung a "Don't Disturb" sign on his door when he turned in. He also warned the telephone operator that he would accept no calls from anyone, except, of course, Mike Hanlon.

Hanlon didn't call. Bugs got a solid ten hours of sound sleep, awakening about six in the evening. He yawned and stretched luxuriously. He squirmed against the pillows, grinning with contentment. And then remembering his resolutions and the dangers they were meant to forefend—he almost flung himself from the bed.

He bathed, shaved, and dressed. By seven o'clock, he had finished his dinner in the coffee shop and was out of the hotel.

And it would be a good four hours before he was due on the job.

He'd already seen the picture playing at the local movie house. He had no money to waste on gambling, even if he had been inclined toward such diversions. And nothing can be more wearisome than simply driving or walking around, with no objective in mind.

So he stepped into a drugstore and called Amy Standish's house. He wanted to see her; he had meant to, he guessed, from the moment he had waked up. He had a feeling that being with her again would do much toward expunging the memory of his session with Joyce Hanlon.

She didn't answer the phone. He hung up with an annoyed sense of having been mistreated. He could be like that, almost childish. Once he decided to do something, he wanted to do it right then. And he was unreasonably affronted if he couldn't.

She'd said he could see her again, hadn't she? Well, why couldn't he then? Why didn't she stay at home like she ought to?

He walked around for a half-hour, and called again. Still no answer. Smoldering and stubborn, he continued to call at thirty-minute intervals. And, finally, a few minutes after ten o'clock, she answered the phone.

By that time, of course, it was too late to see her. To do anything more, that is, than get out to her house before he had to turn around and come back.

"Oh, Mr. McK—Mac," she said, *and was there or was there not a trace of disappointment in her voice?* "Were you trying to get me a little while ago?"

"Probably. Been trying to get you all evening," Bugs grunted.

"Oh, I'm sorry. I'd just stepped in the door, and I got to the phone just as fast as I could, but—"

"It doesn't matter," Bugs cut in gruffly. "I just thought we might have got together for a soda or a drink or something. Ridden around a little while. But I suppose you probably enjoyed yourself a lot more with—doing something else."

The phone went silent. Quiet with rebuke, or indecision. Then, she spoke, not with coolness, perhaps, but something not too distantly akin to it.

"I was working, Mac. At the library."

"The library? I thought you were a teacher."

"I am. The library's in the school, and it's only open in the evenings. We teachers have to take turns serving as librarian."

Bugs waited, not knowing quite what to say. Feeling that it was up to her to go on from that point.

At last, he broke the dragging silence with a gruff. "I see. And I suppose you'll be working there tomorrow night, too."

"Yes, as a matter of fact, I will. I have these two nights together."

"I see," Bugs said again. "Okay, forget it. Sorry I bothered you."

He started to slam up the receiver. Her quick cry stopped him, just before it went down on the hook.

"Wait, Mac . . . *Mac!*"

"Yeah? Yeah?" he said quickly. "I'm still here, Amy."

"I was just going to say that I'll be through by nine, or a few minutes after. Just as soon as I can get the patrons out and lock up. If you'd like to meet me then . . ."

"Swell! Fine," Bugs exclaimed. "I mean, yeah, I can do that. I guess that'll be all right."

She drew a quick breath. She frowned; he could hear the frown in her silence, just as he had heard the rebuke. And then—and he knew it as well as he was standing there—she was smiling. It began with her lips, curving them with lovely tenderness. It spread slowly over the heart-shaped face, dimpling her cheeks, gently indenting the laugh lines. And then it was in her eyes, lighting them up as though the sun had arisen behind them. . . .

"Mac," she said. "Mac, you're crazy. . . ."

"Huh? Well, yeah," Bugs admitted sheepishly. "I guess I probably sound like it sometimes."

"Fortunately, I like crazy people. Particularly those named McKenna who work as house detectives. Now, isn't that a happy coincidence?"

Bugs swallowed. A warm pleasantly prickly feeling spread over his hulking body. There were a thousand things he wanted to say, and he couldn't cut loose with one of them.

Amy's voice came over the wire, soft and understanding. "I'm glad you called, Mac. And I'll look forward to seeing you . . . And, now, good night."

And very gently, she broke the connection.

Bugs returned to the hotel, walking on the sidewalk, ostensibly, but seemingly treading on air. It was preposterous to feel that way over a girl who—over Lou Ford's ex-girlfriend, *if* she was his ex. But that was the way he did feel, and nuts to whether it was preposterous or not. In fact, with very little effort, he managed to exclude Ford from his thoughts about her. He could cut that tin-starred lunk out of the picture as completely as though he did not exist. Which, to Bugs's way of thinking, would have improved the world by several thousand per cent.

There were two telephone call-slips in his room box. Two requests that he call Mrs. Hanlon. Bugs ripped them into shreds, dropped them into a sand jar, and started on his nightly rounds.

It was an unusually quiet night. A good night, Bugs supposed, to take Mike Hanlon along with him. Still, there wasn't any rush about it, and he didn't feel like carrying on an extended conversation, as he would have to with Hanlon. So he dropped the idea, and went it alone.

There was a little ruckus on the tenth floor—some poker players in a corner suite. Bugs asked them to quiet down, and, replied to with belligerence, he quieted them. He elbowed one guy across the windpipe. He grabbed another by his necktie and slapped him in the chops. He hustled the remaining two—who had been drinking heavily—into the bathroom, and shoved them under the shower. Then, he gathered up the cards and chips, tossed them down the waste chute, and calmly departed.

That was the only trouble he encountered on his whole tour (although Bugs could hardly regard an incident so innocuous as trouble). Well, there *was* a very small rift in the routine on the sixth floor: A guy was pounding on a door with the butt of his six-shooter, threatening to kill his wife as soon as he got inside. But he was just drunk, and the gun, which Bugs took away from him, proved to be empty. So there was really nothing to get the wind up about.

Nothing else happened. Nothing, that is, that was worth a second thought in Bugs's opinion. By a few minutes after one, he had completed his rounds and was back in the lobby again.

Leslie Eaton was talking on the telephone as he started past the desk. He saw Bugs and gestured to him, silently mouthing a name. Bugs shook his head and went on toward the coffee shop.

Joyce again. Well, let her call all she damned pleased. When she got tired maybe she'd quit. He no longer felt obligated to her. Neither, needless to say, did he feel constrained to be pleasant or polite to her. She was a tramp;

she couldn't lose him his job, do anything at all to hurt him with Hanlon. And she was smart enough to know it.

The night wore on uneventfully. Strolling about the hotel, wandering through the always amazing world that was the back-o'-the-house, Bugs wondered about Westbrook: What had happened to the little man? How had he disappeared so suddenly and completely? And yet, there was really nothing much to wonder about, was there?

The manager had been without hope, convinced that he was thoroughly and finally washed up. As an alcoholic, then, he had taken refuge in booze. Abandoning all else before it could be taken from him—as he was sure it would be. Holing up in some dive where he could drink and drink and drink, until . . .?

It was too bad, Bugs thought sadly. It just went to show that a man shouldn't throw in the sponge too quickly. All Westbrook would have had to do was make a clean breast of things to Hanlon. If he had done that he would still be on the job, none the worse except for an A-1 chewing-out.

There was something else that Bugs wondered about. A riddle which, at last, would no longer be ignored. What had become of the five thousand—or whatever the exact sum was—that Dudley had stolen?

Certainly, the auditor must have had it. Specifically, he had had it in his trousers—their zippered money-belt, rather—from which, he assumed, Bugs had stolen it. You just couldn't account for his attitude in any other way. You couldn't, at least, except by a fantastic stretch of the imagination. And that being the case—

Bugs's thoughts reached this point, and could go no further. So he indulged in some of the aforesaid imagination-stretching . . . Hell, Dudley might have stashed the loot somewhere and forgotten that he had. Or, well, maybe he'd lost it. Or maybe it *wasn't* the dough that he'd gotten so excited about. Maybe he hadn't stolen it, and it had been something else that had made him make that wild lunge at Bugs.

You couldn't be sure . . . could you? The room had been dark. They'd hardly exchanged a half-dozen words. And everything had happened so fast, been over and done with in the space of seconds.

Yeah, Bugs thought, there was bound to be some "simple" explanation for the missing money. Just about had to be. Otherwise . . . well, he wouldn't let himself think about that. He preferred to think about Amy Standish, and this new life he was building for himself. And he did.

He turned in early again that morning. He again hung the "Don't Disturb" sign on his door, and left word to the same effect with the telephone operator.

He got another good day's sleep. He had dinner in his room, and by eight o'clock was on his way out of the hotel. Passing the desk, he saw two white oblongs in his key-box. He grinned sourly and went on, leaving them there . . . A pretty stubborn gal, this Joyce Hanlon. Well, let her be. It didn't bother him any.

The school—a combination high and grade—was on the immediate outskirts of town, adjoining the brief blocks of houses which comprised the "old family" section. Bugs idly circled the ancient red-brick structure. Then, since it was still well before nine o'clock, he drove back past the austere old houses, looming aloofly in the night like so many box-like fortresses.

Driving as slowly as he could, it took him no more than a couple of minutes. He returned to the school, and parked.

At a minute or so after nine, the double-doors of the school opened and a trickle of people—youngsters and a few adults—came down the walk. A few minutes later, the building lights that had been on went off and Amy came out.

She smiled and squeezed his hand as he helped her into the car. He restarted the motor, asked her where she'd like to go.

"Oh, anywhere. Just so it's not too far. I have to work tomorrow, and I know you don't have much time either."

"Well. Like to turn into town—pick up a couple drinks?"

"No!"—the word came out almost sharply. And then she laughed, with a trace of sadness and apology. "This is a small town, Mac. The people are pretty free and easy about some things, but never their women. And they're the direct opposite of free and easy when it comes to women schoolteachers."

"I see." Bugs yanked the car into gear. "You have to be

careful about your reputation."

"Yes," she said evenly. "I have to be careful about my reputation."

They rode over to the highway, to a recently erected drive-in restaurant. After consulting her stiffly, Bugs ordered malted milks and hamburgers. He had no appetite for the repast, but she ate hers to the last bite and swallow. Gaily, making a joke of it, she even finished the French-fries he had left on his plate.

By then it was ten o'clock, and time to be going. At least, she said timidly, she was afraid she'd have to. "I was up so late the other night, you know, and . . ."

"I know," Bugs grunted. "But that was on a date with Ford. That made it all right."

"Yes. With someone I've known all my life, someone I supposedly was going to marry, it was all right."

"And anything else would be."

"No, *anything* would not. In fact . . ." She left the sentence unfinished, her voice trailing away wearily—and worriedly. Then, she sighed and said, "I'm sorry, Mac. That's about all I can say at this point: that I'm sorry."

"What the hell?" Bugs shrugged. "You don't owe me any explanations."

"No, I don't. Or any apologies, either. I simply said I was sorry because I like you, and I thought it might make you feel better."

Much of Bugs's hurt and anger went away, and his feeling of compassion returned. He stopped the car in front of her house, turned humbly and faced her.

"I'm a dope," he said. "A big fat-headed dope. And you can take that as an apology *and* explanation."

"All right . . ." Her smile came back. "And, Mac, I would like to see you longer than this. Just for an hour or so, it hardly gives us time to say hello, does it? So would you like to come here and have dinner with me tomorrow night?"

"Would I?" Bugs beamed. "But that would be a lot of trouble for you, and—"

"No, it wouldn't. Not in any way. There's a Negro woman who used to work for the folks. I can get her to come in and help, and by the time she's eaten herself and got things cleared up . . ."

He'd be gone. There'd be a third party with them throughout the evening.

She looked at him, obviously anxious but too proud to press the invitation. Choking back his resentment, Bugs said he'd be very glad to come to dinner.

"Then it's all settled. You can come early, around six, and we'll have the whole evening together. And now"—she leaned back in the seat, held her arms out—"If you'd like to kiss me good night, I'd like to have you."

Bugs drew her to him. He kissed her not at all in the way that he wanted to nor in the way that, subconsciously, he felt that he was entitled to. It was no more than a gentle touching of their lips, and his arms were loose around her body.

She drew her head back, studied his hard face dreamily. She brushed a lock of hair from his forehead and said, "Thank you, Mac. Thank you, very much."

"You're thanking *me*? What for?"

"You know. For not spoiling things. For not making me feel that . . . But I knew you wouldn't. You couldn't with eyes as kind as yours."

"Yeah," Bugs said gruffly. "Kind of screwy, you mean."

"I mean, kind, good. Like they had seen so much hurt that they could never cry enough."

"Hell, I never cried in my life."

"Then I think it's about time. And I think you'll be happier when you do. But, anyway . . ." Her voice sank to a drowsy murmur. "Kiss me again, Mac. And, Mac, if you want to do it a little harder . . ."

He kissed her again, a very little harder, only a little less chastely. She thanked him simply, as she had before. And then they said good night and parted.

Bugs drove back to the hotel, very happy and pleased with himself. Ignoring the tiny voice which jeered him for a chump and insisted that he was a sucker.

He felt good. He had a nice thing going here. Why wonder about its niceness, then? Why take it apart to see what made it tick?

He stopped at the desk, and got the stuff out of his box. He almost tore the letter up before he discovered that it was a letter, and not another of Joyce's call-slips.

Absently, his mind still on Amy, he sat down in a corner of the lobby and opened it.

Mr. McKenna: You killed Mr. Dudley. I know you did because I was in the bathroom, and I heard everything that happened. And if you are stubborn or uncooperative, I will see that Mr. Lou Ford knows about it. You have a choice, Mr. McKenna. You can mail five thousand dollars to me, at the address below, or you can go to jail—perhaps, to the electric chair. Naturally, I'd prefer that you did the former, since telling what I know would necessarily be embarrassing for me, and would make me nothing. But I will do it, if I don't get the money. The choice is up to you, Mr. McKenna. Better not delay in making it.

> Jean Brown,
> c/o General Delivery
> Westex City, Texas.

The letter was printed neatly in pencil; the text as well as the address on the envelope. It was postmarked Westex City, but that was just a dodge, of course. The blackmailer was right here in the Hanlon, someone who had been on intimate terms with Dudley, and who knew enough about him, Bugs, to know that he had two strikes against him.

It had to be. Also, considering the circumstances of the blackmailer's rendezvous with Dudley, it just about had to be a woman. One of two women. For Bugs could think of only two with the necessary qualifications. Both would have some knowledge of his past. Both would have or could have known Dudley well. Both could come and go about the hotel without attracting attention.

Joyce Hanlon? Well, she was capable of it, all right. And it would perfectly suit her purposes to swing a club like this at him. She wouldn't actually want the money, of course. It would simply be a means of making him sweat, crowding him into a corner. Then she would step in and offer him a way out.

Unfortunately—unfortunately since Bugs wanted her to be the culprit—he knew that Joyce could not have been the lady in the bathroom. He'd talked to her seconds after Dudley's tumble from the window. She couldn't possibly have got from Dudley's room to her own in time to receive that call.

So that left Rosalie Vara; she had to be it. Rosie whom he had always liked and gone out of his way to be nice to.

She'd gotten the five grand, and now . . . Well, maybe Dudley had kidded her that he had more, another five. Or maybe she was just making the old college try.

A man may not have much, but he's apt to bust a gut getting it. *If* it seems the only way to stay out of jail or the chair.

Bugs shredded and re-shredded the letter, and dropped it into a sand jar. He guessed he must have kind of been expecting something like this—although not from Rosie. Because he was worried, naturally, but not greatly surprised. This was the kind of lousy break he always got. It would have been damned strange if he got anything else.

But he'd smartened up a lot since his last bad break. And he had a lot more to fight for than he used to have. So maybe he'd wind up catching it in the neck again—catching it worse than he ever had before—but he sure as hell didn't plan to. What he planned (and the details were already forming in his mind) was something else entirely.

Rosie . . .

Slowly, his eyes lifted up to the mezzanine, seeking her, then shifted to the huge square-faced clock at the head of the lobby.

Eleven-thirty. She'd be, or should be, up on the room floors at this time.

Bugs pushed himself up from his chair. He strolled over to the elevator bank and ascended to the twelfth floor. He was very calm, casual. Maybe, he guessed, the full implications of his predicament hadn't had time to register on him. Or it could be that he found it hard to feel anything much toward Rosie but hurt and irritation. At any rate, he had seldom been calmer, more sure of himself, in his life.

She had admitted herself to his room with her maid's key, and was now busily at work. Bugs got some cigarettes and a clean handkerchief out of his dresser drawer, said that, yes, he had been getting out of the room early the last couple of nights.

"Figured I was getting stale, y'know, just eating and sleeping and working. I'm going to try getting out a lot more, from now on."

"Well, now, I think you should, Mr. McKenna," she nodded seriously. "This night work . . . well, of course, I'm very happy in my job. But I do find myself getting into a rut."

It was an opening, she'd handed it to him herself. Casually, Bugs moved into it. "You get that way, too, huh? Well, look, I'm driving over to Westex City the day after tomorrow. Pulling out right after work. How about coming along with me?"

"*With you?*" She gave a start. "But—but—"

"Fellow I've got to see a few miles the other side of Westex. Owns a lot of property in that section. I'm having him rush me some money tomorrow, so I'll have to go over and fix up a note or something."

"But . . . well, that's awfully nice of you to ask me, Mr. McKenna. But I—"

"I could drop you off there in town, and pick you up in a couple of hours. Don't suppose it would be very exciting for you; just the ride and lunch. But—"

"Mr. McKenna," she said. "Mr. McKenna. . ."

"Yeah?"

"I don't think I'd better. There isn't as much prejudice here in the Southwest as there is in the South, but I am a Negro, and—"

"So what?" Bugs shrugged. "You don't look like one. You won't be wearing a sign on your back."

Her eyes flashed; her lips came together in a proudly angry line. Because even for Bugs McKenna, the statement set a new high or low for tactlessness. And, yet, maybe it was that tactlessness—the apparently complete lack of guile—that turned the trick.

She stared at him a moment, eyes narrowed, lips compressed. Bugs looked back at her, the very picture of innocence personified. And, suddenly, she was laughing, bubbling over with delicious amusement.

"All right, Mr. McKenna." She dabbed at her eyes. "I'd like to go very much, if you're sure you want me. And as you say, I won't have a sign on my back."

"Now, I didn't mean that like it sounded," Bugs said, sheepishly. "I—"

"I know. I know how you mean it. . . .The day after tomorrow, you said?"

"That's right. I've got an appointment here in town tomorrow. Anyway, I have to be here to receive the money this fellow's sending me."

It went over perfectly, it seemed to Bugs. She left and he locked the door and sat down at his writing desk.

He took a half-dozen sheets of stationery from the drawer, tore them into crude oblongs. He stuffed them into a lettersize envelope, and stamped and addressed it. Later that night, he mailed it at a box outside of the hotel.

The night passed in the usual manner of his nights. Retiring at the end of his shift, he followed the routine of the previous two mornings. It wouldn't work indefinitely, he guessed. Joyce was a very determined dame, and she was playing for big stakes. So, sooner or later, she'd start pressing. She'd ignore that sign on his door, or insist that the operators put her calls through.

But . . . first things first. He'd take care of her when the time came. Right now, there were other things to be taken care of.

He arose at five o'clock, was on his way in thirty minutes. There were a couple of call-slips in his box—and he leaned over the desk to make sure they were call-slips. Leaving them in the box, he went out the doors to the street.

He bought a bouquet of flowers, the best that five dollars would buy. Also, after a little mental calculation, he bought a one-pound box of candy. Carrying these modest burdens, he knocked on Amy Standish's door at five minutes of six.

He knocked. He knocked and knocked. He noticed for the first time that all the shades were drawn, that there was no sound of activity in the house. He hesitated, uneasily, wondering if he could possibly have got mixed up on the invitation; whether it had been for tonight or some other night.

And the door cracked open an inch, and Amy spoke to

him through the crevice. "Mac"—her voice sounded muf-
fled, choked up. "What are you—? Didn't you get my message?"

"Message? Oh," Bugs said, remembering. "Well, I guess
there was one in my box. But—"

"I'm sorry. We'll have to make it some other night, Mac."

"But look, what's the matter?" Bugs protested. "What's
wrong? Did I do something that—"

"No, it's nothing you did. I—I can't talk about it now,
Mac. Now, if you'll excuse me . . . *please*, Mac . . ."

Bugs persisted stubbornly. Hell, if she was sick or something, he wanted to know about it. Suddenly her voice
cracked, rose hysterically.

"I said to go on! Leave me alone! I've told you and told
you that I c-can't talk, and if you had any sense you'd—
you'd . . . ."

The door slammed in his face. Bugs glowered at it furiously. Then, he flung the candy and flowers to the porch
and stamped back to the car.

He had a very bad time with himself for the next few
hours. Disappointment mingled with anger, and anger
with hurt. And . . . it was a very bad time. So bad that it
burned itself out before much of the night had elapsed, and
he could reason and be reasonable.

Of course, there was no excuse for what Amy had done.
Couldn't be any that he could think of. Still, she had doubtless thought she had a reason for standing him up, even if
she didn't have. And no matter how sore he was—or had
been—he couldn't see her pulling such stunts for the hell of
it. To see, that is, how much she could get away with.
She'd been badly upset, too. She hadn't liked it any better
than he did.

He became reasonably placid again, reasonably at peace
with himself. By the end of his shift, he had firmly decided
to forgive Amy . . . provided, naturally, that she was properly contrite, and that she satisfactorily explained her
actions.

. . . He picked up Rosalie Vara a couple blocks from the
hotel. He had previously purchased a couple of containers
of coffee and some sweet rolls, and they ate breakfast as

they rode. Neither did much talking. Rosalie seemed very tired from her night's work, and Bugs was reluctant to talk. In view of what he had to do—and what she was doing to him—even maintaining a decent silence was an almost intolerable strain.

Westex City was a city in fact as well as name. Not a large one—the population was under fifty thousand—but one that was prosperous and important, since it was the field headquarters for various oil companies.

It was less than sixty miles from Ragtown. But what with the narrow highway and the heavy traffic, it was almost eleven when Bugs and Rosalie arrived. He made arrangements for meeting her later—entirely unnecessary arrangements, he thought grimly—and asked where she would like to be let out. She said politely that any place in the business district would be fine, so he dropped her off seven or eight blocks from the post office.

He drove on, as though he were heading out of town. then, after a block or so, he whipped around a corner and sped back toward the business section.

He found a suitable parking place. A side-street spot which was near his destination and hers. He left the car in it, hastened up to the main thoroughfare, and entered a restaurant.

It was directly across from the post office. Seated a few stools down the counter, he could see both entrances of the building.

If he had been less intent on those entrances, if say, he had taken a good look around the restaurant, he might have seen—

But, no, probably he wouldn't have. The place was expensive, pretentious, dimly lit in the sometime fashion of such places. So, even if he had looked around, it is doubtful that he would have seen the two people in the distant rear booth.

But he could be seen. Not by Amy Standish, since her back was to the entrance. But Lou Ford, seated on the opposite bench, could see him perfectly.

He gave no sign of the fact to Amy, made no mention of Bugs's presence. He went on with his meal, drawling idly, grinning at the girl's bitter or dispirited rejoinders. But he was watching interestedly, noting Bugs's watchfulness, the course of his intent stare. And so he saw what Bugs saw. And when Bugs jumped up and left the restaurant, he also arose.

Bugs had given her a couple of minutes inside the post office. He reached the entrance just as she was coming out of it, shoving something into her purse. And her eyes widened, and she stopped dead in her tracks.

"Why, Mr. McKenna," she faltered. "What . . . I thought that—"

"I know what you thought!" Bugs gripped her by the arm. "Come on!"

"But—" Her trembling smile fell apart. She held back fearfully. "B-but—what have I done? Why are you—?"

"I'm warning you, Rosie!" Bugs gritted. "I don't want to hurt you, but if you don't move I'll move you. I'll rip that arm right off you!"

She held back a moment longer, started to say something else. Then, all the spirit seemed to go out of her, all the quiet pride and self-assurance. And she went with him meekly.

He hustled her back to his car. He shoved her into it roughly, crowded in at her side. She was crying a little now, pressing her fingers against her eyes to hold back the tears.

Bugs took here purse, and yanked it open. . . .

The place was a few miles outside of Ragtown; there are places like it near almost every town and city. Areas densely overgown with trees, cluttered with shrubs and bushes, laced with a winding maze of footpaths and car tracks. They are isolated, yet easily accessible. They have various names, all carrying the same slyly lewd connotation.

. . . The two "girls"—women of about thirty—had draped their clothes over some convenient tree limbs. Now, stripped to their slips, they shivered in the chilly

West Texas morning.

"Wonder what's keeping those guys?" grumbled the girl called Peg. "Why the hell couldn't they undress here, like we did?"

"Now, honey," murmured her companion, Gladys. "Real swell fellas like that, you can't ask a lot of questions. You don't find guys every day that pop for twenty bucks."

"Yeah. I guess . . . You s'pose our purses are all right in the car, Glad?"

"Why not? The fellas are lockin' it up tight, aren't they?"

"Well, I wish I'd brought my coat with me, anyhow. I paid five hundred bucks for that hunk of fur, and—"

"And what did I pay for mine, hon? Exactly the same, wasn't it? We both started saving for 'em at the same time. Now, you know we wouldn't want to drag those nice coats around these bushes."

"But I'm cold, darn it! I'm absolutely freezing!"

"Well, now, you won't be very long, hon. The fellas are bound to—"

The sudden roar of a motor drowned out her sentence. A lessening roar as a car was slammed into gear and driven away. The girls looked at each other dumbfounded. They broke into curses, scampered a few futile steps in pursuit. Then, weeping, they fell into one another's arms.

Ed and Ted Gusick were stripping the purses as they drove. Slowing down, they tossed them into the bushes, then gathered speed again. And then, as they neared the highway, Ted suddenly slammed on the brakes.

A man had stumbled out of the underbrush, tumbled directly in the path of their car. He lurched to his feet again—a man in shape only—a ragged, bedraggled, stinking bundle of filth. Cursing frightfully, he wobbled toward them.

"Friggers! Caught you, didn't I? Up'n the goddamned floor, an' no friggin' around about it!"

"Listen, Mr. Westbrook . . ." Ted and Ed eased out of the car, watching him cautiously. "It's me—you know, Ted Gusick. And here's Ed, right here with me. Now—"

"No 'scuses!" Westbrook bellowed. "Makes no difference who y'are. Either y'cut the stuff'r—I'll show you, by God!"

He came at them in a rush. Ted tripped him nimbly. Ed

caught him under the arms, and lowered him gently to the ground.

He began to cry, sobbing out curses as the tears streamed down his bristled, filth-smeared face. Ed looked worriedly at his brother.

"Jesus," he whispered. "What are we gonna do with him, Ted?"

"Do with him? Why, we're gonna take him with us, you jerk."

"But—what then? I mean, what are we gonna *do*?"

Ted didn't have the slightest idea. Being at a loss for one—and in typical Gusick fashion—he responded with a kind of self-righteous abuse.

"I suppose you want to leave him here, you rotten son-of-a-bitch! Just walk off and leave a fine man like Mr. Westbrook. Well, I always thought you were pretty god-damned low-down, and now by God, I know it!"

He swung irritably, landing a painful punch in Ed's ribs. Ed swung, with identical results. These formalities dispensed with, they loaded Westbrook into their car, made him peaceful with a gently expert tap on the button and drove off.

They lived in the old-family section of town, in an excellent apartment, which, before its transformation, had been the loft of the family barn. The building was on an alley, a good two hundred feet removed from the house. The lower floor was boarded up, and the only entrance to their apartment was from the alley. Briefly, they could just about do as they pleased, come and go as they pleased, without being heard or observed. And lovers of privacy that they were—for reasons which need not be gone into—they were delighted to pay the boom-town rental of three hundred dollars a month.

They got Westbrook up the stairs unseen and installed him in the master bedroom. They bathed him, fed him, waited on and catered to him; and they continued to do so from that day on.

They got him through the d.t.'s with drugs pilfered from the hotel doctor. They doled out drinks to him, trying to taper him off the binge. They were partially successful in this, getting him down to a mere few pints a day. But even this relatively small amount, combined with Westbrook's totally hopeless outlook, was enough to keep him sodden. He had nothing to hang on to. Nothing to go forward or back to. So he succumbed to the booze, accepted its deadening and deadly embrace without resistance.

Ted and Ed pleaded with him. They declared—as they believed—that he was the best damned hotel man in the country; one of the few real hotel men left—and if he'd just pull himself together . . .

Things were going to pot at the Hanlon. A new manager had lasted just one day, and now old Mike was trying to swing the job himself, with the help of the chief clerk. And, brother, were they bitching up the joint! He'd be tickled to death to get Mr. Westbrook back, if he'd just get off the goddammed whiz. So—so how about it, huh, Mr. Westbrook. Get right off it, huh, sir, and everything'll be swell.

Westbrook wept babyishly, charging them with prevarication and boobishness. Then, getting a grip on himself, he lashed them with ear-purpling profanity. He would do something, all right! He would keep them under the closest observation, see to it that they did not cut his throat and steal his clothes, as, indubitably, they planned on doing.

He would see to it that they conducted themselves properly while in his presence; that never in any way did they give any outward manifestation of their pimpish, thieving, shiftless, impertinent and generally bastardly souls. They would tell him no more of their goddamned lies about the hotel—and anything they said *would* be a goddamned lie. He had put up with them as long as he intended to, and from now on, by God, they would toe the mark, or he personally would kick the crap out of them.

"And I can do it, get me?"—this with a belligerently red-eyed glare. "You think I can't, just give me a little more trouble."

"Yes, sir. Certainly, sir, Mr. Westbrook."

"All right, then. Open 'nother bottle, and be quick about it!"

They obeyed. They continued to. In their feudal minds, the fact that a liege-lord had lost his sanity did not lose him the right to reign. He was still the boss. He was authority. He was a symbol of something which, far more than the socially enlightened, the Ted and Ed Gusicks find necessary to existence.

During the day, they took turns about waiting on him. Before departing for work at night, they set out whiskey, food, and cigarettes, everything he might need or want, or think he needed or wanted. And never again did they mention the hotel in his presence. He had told them not to. Moreover, in his increasingly sodden state, it had become impossible to talk to him.

One night, or, rather, very early one morning, Westbrook awakened with a feeling of having been reborn. His head was entirely clear. There was none of the hideous shaking, the gut-wracking nausea, which normally accompanied his awakenings.

Actually, he was in a state of euphoria. Nature was giving him one last unhampered whirl at life before closing in for the kill. But the sense of optimism and well-being seemed entirely valid, and while it lasted he dumped every bottle of his liquor into the toilet.

He had scarcely done so when he was plunged back into the abyss: to a far deeper depth than he had previously penetrated. A convulsion wracked him, doubled him with terror and pain. Invisible hands gripped his head, squeezing tighter and tighter and still tighter, until his brain squirmed and screamed in agony.

He looked around wildly. He saw the empty bottles on the floor, and had no memory of how they had got there.

Ted and Ed, he thought. It was they who had done this to him. They'd been after him to stop drinking, and now—

"Kill 'em," he mumbled fiercely. "Kill 'em, kill 'em, kill 'em. I—I got to have something. I—I GOT TO HAVE—"

Staggering into the kitchen, he pawed frantically through the cupboards. He went from room to room, jerking out drawers, knocking over furniture, upturning cushions and mattresses. In the bathroom medicine cabinet, he found a pint bottle of rubbing alcohol. He clutched it to his breast and staggered back into the kitchen.

He set a small pan on the work shelf. He held a stack of bread over it, started to filter the alcohol through the bread. And his hand jerked convulsively, crashing the bottle against the wall.

He screamed, sobbed, over the terrible loss. For a moment he was too dispirited and hopeless to go on. Then he jerked open the refrigerator, and began jerking out its contents.

There was nothing in it. Nothing, Westbrook thought angrily, but crap: food. The bastards! Oh, those fiendish, sneaky bastards! They'd loaded their refrigerator with eggs and butter and milk and cream, and steaks and roasts and—dozens of worthless items. And not a lousy, wonderful drop to drink.

"Kill 'em," Westbrook babbled. "Kill 'em. If it's the last thing I ever do. I'll—I'll—"

Back in the rear of the refrigerator, concealed until now by a bag of grapefruit, was a bottle. A jug-like, gift-type carafe filled with a chocolatey liquid. It would be syrup, of course. They had guessed that he would be dying, by now, and had planned this ultimate and unbearable disappointment to shove him over the brink.

Westbrook thrust his head inside the refrigerator, scraping his ears in the process. Squinting, the print wavering and blurring before his eyes, he read the label on the bottle.

Creme de Cacao! A full fifth—minus a sip or so—of seventy-proof liqueur!

Westbrook let out a low moan. He started to grab for it; then, remembering the horrible accident with the alcohol, he held a pan against the shelf, and raked the bottle into it. He put the pan on the floor. He tilted the bottle on its side, and pulled the cork.

There was a gentle gurgle, a rich brown flow. Whimpering, Westbrook reached for a teacup. He wasn't risking the loss of a drop of this. *They* might fool him once, by God, but they couldn't do it twice. He'd get it all out into the pan, and—

The flow stopped. Something inside the bottle had lodged in its neck. Westbrook moaned piteously. Somehow, he managed to nip the obstruction between a trembling thumb and forefinger, and yanked it out.

The wonderful gurgling resumed. Westbrook tilted the bottle, cautiously assisting the flow. Finally, his patience exhausted, he snatched it up, shook out the few remaining drops and hurled it into the corner.

And then, at last, he drank.

He drank two full cups, one after the other. Cheeks puffed, eyes bulging, he shuddered violently. He sighed and leaned back against the refrigerator, breathing in long, deep, grateful breaths.

He got a cigarette lighted. Picking up the pan—and he could trust his hands now—he started to fill his cup again.

Something plopped into it. The object that had stopped up the neck of the bottle. Gingerly, he got it between two fingers, examined it, frowning.

It wasn't a cork, as he had thought. It was a small balloon, stuffed tightly with something, and its end closed with a rubber band.

A premonitious shiver ran through Westbrook. He wiped the thing off with his handkerchief, wiped his fingers clean, and ripped open the balloon.

The "stuffing" fell to the floor. It consisted of currency, a tightly rolled wad of five-hundred-dollar bills. He counted them, and a low yowl of mingled triumph and outrage spewed through his teeth.

Outrage, yes. For while he didn't know how they'd latched onto this dough, he knew damned well where it had come from. Dudley had been short five grand and here *was* five grand. And if they hadn't stolen it from him—the selfsame sum that he had pinched—who had they stolen it from? And if it wasn't stolen—laughable thought!—if it wasn't too hot to handle, why had they hidden it so carefully?

The questions were nonsensically elementary; their answers axiomatic to a man of Westbrook's background. He thought of the terror and hopelessness he had lived in because of the theft, and his lips parted in another yowl.

"Now, I *am* going to do it," he vowed grimly. "Now, I *will* kill them!"

There was a supply of clean shirts, underclothing and the like in his bedroom; and his suit, unworn since he had moved in here, was also cleaned and pressed. He bathed and shaved, dressed himself meticulously. He made and drank a pot of coffee, casually kicking the creme de cacao pan out of his way.

Alcohol. Why had he ever   wanted the stuff? What could

it give him that he didn't have, or could easily get? Well, no matter. He didn't want it now, and he had a strange conviction that he would never want it again.

He finished the coffee. Then he began prowling through the apartment; looking in closets and on shelves. Studying various maneuverable objects.

He took his time about it, and at last he found exactly what he was looking for: a heavy wooden rod, some three inches in circumference and approximately four feet long.

It was installed in a closet where it served as a clothes hanger rack. Ripping it out, he took a few practice swings with it, and grimly satisfied, returned to the living room.

This would do the trick, he thought. He wouldn't quite kill those bastards, but he'd make them think they'd been killed. He'd—

"God!" he said suddenly, "God!"—he flung the pole from him. "What's the matter with me? What's been the matter with me?"

And when the Gusicks arrived from work, he only talked to them.

There was nothing funny about theft, he said. It was not amusing or shrewd or sharp, ever to inflict pain or loss upon another. And it was the job of everyone—not just the individual affected—to see that no one suffered preventable pain or loss. You had to do it. Otherwise you had no peace; you had constantly to keep your guard up. And when you wearied, as you inevitably must, you got it in the neck yourself.

He liked them, he went on. In many ways he was deeply indebted to them. They were sharp and on their toes—and he liked that. But if they were to work under him again, they had better be sharp in the right way. And he hoped he'd made it clear what the right way was.

That was what he said, in substance. Having said it, and clutching the money tightly in his pocket, he returned to the hotel.

But this, as has been indicated, was days after Dudley's death.

And the fate of Bugs McKenna—and various other parties—had already been settled.

13

There was nothing incriminating in Rosalie Vara's purse, and nothing on her personally. He had searched her briefly but efficiently—and God, how he hated himself for it now!—and all he had found in her clothes was Rosalie.

She had gone to the post office for an entirely innocent reason, and the evidence was in his hands. He went on staring at it, the postcard he had found in her purse; feeling stupider and stupider, feeling his face grow redder and redder. He didn't know what to say to her. He was afraid to look at her. So he kept his eyes on the card:

> Dear Rose:
> Sure was glad and surprised to get your telephone call today, and sure wish I could see you. But like I told you, I had to check with my boss, and he says he is going to need me straight on through until six o'clock. So unless you're going to be in town that late, I guess we can't get together. Sure sorry Rose. Let me know a little more ahead of time when you're coming over again. Love, Ella Mae.

Bugs could stare at the card no longer. Awkwardly, he laid it in her lap; gave her a sidewise miserable glance. She was wearing a crisp linen suit, with a starched white shirtwaist. Her small, beautifully arched feet were shod in high-heeled canvas-like pumps. A wisp of a hat, pert and attractive but with the indefinable stamp of the homemade, perched atop the glossy smooth-lying thickness of her coal-black hair.

It was a cheap outfit, very low-priced at least. Charming and chic only because she wore it, and because of the hours that must have gone into its selection and preparation.

And this was supposed to have been his blackmailer! This was supposed to be a common tart, a gal who would hustle a fast buck in a guy's bedroom! This, this quietly good-mannered young woman who was so honest that she announced, unnecessarily and to her undeniable disadvantage, that she was a Negro!

Well, sure. The postcard didn't absolutely establish her innocence. She might have planted it herself, suspecting that he intended to trap her. She might have, could have, but he knew damned well she hadn't. Everything about her contradicted the theory.

She'd liked him, as he had liked her. Right from the beginning. So she had accepted his invitation, got herself all tyked out in her Sunday's best, tried to arrange a meeting with her girl friend, thus tactfully freeing him of any necessity to entertain her. And he had repaid all this by—

"Rose," he said. "I wish I could tell you how sorry I am, Rosie."

"It's q-quite all right." Her lips trembled. "After all, you don't have to apologize or explain to anyone in my position. You can do anything you want to, and if they don't like it—"

"Don't. Don't, Rosie," he begged. "You know I'm not like that."

"W-well. I certainly never thought you were. I thought . . . s-something awfully foolish, I guess. That, you asked me to come with you as a mark of respect. T-that you were saying we were f-friends, and you weren't ashamed to—to—"

Her eyes brimmed. Sobbing, she turned suddenly, and buried her face against his shoulder.

"I f-feel so dirty. So degraded. Like there was just no use in—in—"

"You mustn't." Bugs patted the small square shoulders. "I was just gagging, see? I mean, a guy's been pulling a gag on me, and I thought maybe—"

" . . .t-took me back to something I thought I'd forgotten. To a time in Chicago years ago. A man struck up a conversation with me on a streetcar, and he seemed very nice. So—"

The guy had gotten off the car with her. He'd grabbed her purse suddenly, and shoved a five-dollar bill into it. Kept possession of it while he whistled up a prowl car. A vice dick, yeah. One on the make like a lot of them were. So he'd fallen for her, he said. And if she'd like to stay out of the can, keep from getting a police record, why he was willing . . .

Bugs listened hard-faced, sharing her heartbreak. He said again that the post office thing had been in the nature of a gag. He couldn't explain it just now. But—

"Aw, go on"—Lou Ford peered through the window. "Sounds like it'd be real amusin'."

Bugs gave a start, and Rose drew away from him quickly. Scowling, he snarled a question at the deputy.

"What am I doin' here?" Ford said. "Well, now, what would I be doin' here? Banking some dough maybe? Investin' some of my ill-gotten gains? . . . How does that sound to you?"

"I'll buy it!"

"Like it, huh? Figured you probably would. Yes sir, I plain counted on it, and that's a fact. But maybe that ain't the real reason. I ain't sayin' it is or it ain't, but let's just suppose. Suppose I said I was here to keep an eye on you?"

Bugs snorted, laughed hollowly. Ford beamed at him.

"Like that even better, do you? Really rubs you on the funny bone. Well, maybe we ought to take it a couple hops further down the trail then. Let's say the reason I was keepin' an eye on you was because I thought you might do a runout. And the reason I thought that—let's say—is because I thought you'd killed a guy and robbed him of five thousand dollars."

The deputy waited, grinning widely. He had the air of one who has sprung a delightful joke.

"You don't think that's funny?" he said. "It don't tickle you, a-tall?"

"I don't know what you're talking about," Bugs grunted. "Where'd you get the idea that Dudley had five thousand dollars?"

"Well, it wasn't too hard to come by. Hotel's got lots of employees. Employees all got mouths. And I got a couple of ears, just in case you hadn't noticed. They ain't as good as yours maybe, don't hear somethin' that ain't said, and— And I didn't mention Dudley's name, Bugs. I didn't say it was Dudley that had the five thousand."

Bugs shrugged. He'd seen his mistake the second he made it. "Hell," he said casually. "He's the only guy that's died recently that I know of. I figured you had to be talking about him."

"Yeah? Well"—Ford moved his head in a judicious nod. "Ought to give you an *A* for sharpness, anyhow. Or maybe an *A-minus*. Can't hardly give you a perfect score when you ain't introduced me to your lady friend."

"What makes you think she wants to be introduced to you?" Bugs snapped. But he curtly performed the introductions.

Rosalie murmured a polite acknowledgement. Ford leaned further through the window, studying her interestedly.

"Believe I've seen you before, ain't I? Look a lot prettier in them street clothes, but—"

"Thank you," said Rosalie. "Yes, sir, I work at the hotel."

"Mmm-hmm. Night maid, right? Did you make up Dudleys' room when he was alive?"

"No, sir. He worked days so his room would be done by one of the day maids."

"But you got up around that way at night. Could have dropped in on him easy enough."

"Yes, sir, I could have. But I never did. I had no reason to."

"Real sure about that? Sure you didn't have about five thousand reasons to?"

"Five thou—!" She gave him a startled look. "But—but, Mr. Ford. You surely don't think that I—"

"No, he doesn't think it?" Bugs cut in angrily. "This is just his way of amusing himself. It gives him something to do between shakedowns."

Ford winked at him. He said maybe he'd give Bugs that *A* for sharpness after all. "But gettin' back to the subject . . . Ever use any chloral hydrate, Miss Vara? I don't mean did you ever take any personally. Just if you used it."

"Why, I—I don't believe so. I'm afraid I don't even know what it is."

"Well, maybe you don't know it by that name. Maybe you'd call it knock-out drops, or—"

"Knock-out drops? But how—w-why would I—"

"You wouldn't," Bugs said, "and he knows it! Now, what are you getting at, Ford? What's chloral got to do with Dudley?"

"I didn't tell you? Well, now I guess it plumb slipped my mind," Ford drawled. "Dudley had a whoppin' load of it in his innards. Enough to coldcock a cow. The doc figures it'd've killed him if he hadn't gone out the window first."

"But—"

"Kind of knocks the suicide idea in the head, don't it? Makes everything as confusin' as—excuse me, Miss Vara—all hell. There wasn't none of the stuff in his room, so we know someone slipped it to him. But if they was gettin' home that way, why bother with the window deal? They didn't have to. The guy'd have been out cold inside of five or ten minutes and anyone who knew anything about chloral hydrate would know it."

"Well . . ." Bugs couldn't think. A great burden had slipped from his conscience, and his one thought was that Dudley would have died regardless of the scuffle between them. "Well, I suppose this person, whoever he was—"

"She, you mean, don't you? It's a woman's weapon, and a woman'd have the best chance of slipping it to him."

"She, then. I'd say she pushed him out the window—if he was pushed—to cover up on the chloral. You know, to make it look like a suicide instead of murder."

"That'd make her pretty stupid, wouldn't it? Even half-way bright, she'd know that an autopsy was a cinch."

"So she was stupid," Bugs said. "So are a lot of people."

He had seen Amy at last, standing in a nearby doorway. He caught her eye, and she smiled uncomfortably, disclaiming connection with the situation with an embarrassed gesture.

He looked away from her coldly, turning to Ford. "You don't really suspect Miss Vara. You have no reason to. But she's answered all your questions, and—"

"Uh-uh. 'Fraid you're wrong there," Ford said. "Ain't begun to ask 'em all."

"Then ask them back in Ragtown! Follow along behind us, if you want to but we're leaving. I've had enough, by God! I'm not going to sit here while you pull your clown act on Miss Vara. And she's not going to sit here and take it. We—"

"You mean you don't like sittin' here?" Ford's eyebrows went up. "Well, now, I thought it was right comfortable.

But o'course if you'd rather go down to the jail . . . That's right, yep," he nodded, "You're still in my county."

"But—" Bugs choked up with fury. "What's it all about, for God's sake? Why are you—"

"Now, dogged if it don't look like you're gettin all excited," Ford said. "Miss Vara, maybe we ought to do our talkin' out on the walk."

"She's not doing any more talking. We're going," Bugs said.

"Wouldn't be much point to it. Doubt if you get six blocks before a squad car brought you back. Hardly figure it's worth doin', do you, Miss Vara?"

Rosalie didn't answer him. She simply opened the door quickly and got out. Ford strolled around the car and joined her on the walk.

"Now which-all rooms do you make up at night, Miss Vara? Besides Mr. McKenna's, that is."

"Well, the other night workers sleep out, so his would be the only one I do regularly. But there are always a few others—not always the same ones on the same nights—that I occasionally make up."

"Uh-huh?"

"Mr. and Mrs. Hanlon, for example. Mr. Hanlon particularly. He frequently doesn't go to sleep before morning because of the pain he's in, and . . ."

Bugs got out of the car. He asked what the hell Ford was pulling. "If your questions are so damned important, why didn't you ask them sooner? Why did you wait until now? Why did you just let everything slide until now, and then—"

"Could be I wasn't ready until now," Ford said blandly. "What's wrong with now, anyways?"

"Everything! Miss Vara's—she's had a hard day, and she doesn't feel well. And we both have to work tonight. *Work,* understand? W-o-r-k! We're working tonight, and if we don't get back and—"

"W-o-r-k, eh?" Ford said. "Now, I always thought you spelled it with a *u.* Fella learns somethin' new every day, don't he?"

"Now, dammit, Ford . . ."

"But I see your point, got to be gettin' in your beauty sleep. Can't say that Miss Vara stands in need of any more beauty-in', but I can see where you . . ." He broke off grinning, beckoned without turning around. "Amy, girl. Come on over."

Amy came forward reluctantly. Lou Ford gave her a jovial nudge toward Bugs.

"Got some talkin' to do to Miss Vara, here," he explained. "But her and Bugs have got to be gettin' back. So I figure maybe you better ride with him, and she can just come along with me."

"Now, really, Lou"—Amy's shamed eyes dropped. "I'd be glad to ride with Mac, of course, but—"

"Miss Vara's riding with me," Bugs said bluntly. "I brought her here, and—"

"No, please!" Rosalie gave him a quick smile. "It's perfectly all right. Mr. McKenna. Let's do as Mr. Ford says."

Bugs hesitated, assented surlily. There was nothing else to do that he could see. As Ford and Rosalie departed, he yanked the car door open, grunted a rude invitation to Amy Standish.

"Thank you," she said. "I think I'd better take a bus."

"Oh, come on, dammit! If I'm willing, why—"

"Yes, why?" she cut in shakily. "Why should I do anything but grovel with gratitude? You can get upset and lose your temper and act just as nasty as you know how, and that's all right! That's your privilege and I'm just supposed to put up with it. I'm not supposed to have any feelings! I'm not supposed to feel any humiliation! I'm not entitled to any c-courtesy or u-understanding or—"

She was about to cry, Bugs observed with an inward groan. God, he'd already had one crying woman on his hands today, and a woman in tears was one thing that had always got him. He just couldn't take it. And he didn't want to hurt Amy. His feelings about her might be pretty mixed up, but he certainly didn't want her hurt.

So he apologized profusely. He got her into the car, and they headed for Ragtown. The traffic was even heavier now than it had been in the morning. The around-the-clock oilfield shifts were changing, and the cars of the workmen vied with the mammoth trucks and tractors for space on the highway.

It was impossible to make any time. Bugs finally gave up

trying to. Idling along between two trucks, he slanted a glance at Amy, caught her studying him with a peculiar expression on her face.

It vanished instantly. Looking straight ahead, she remarked that Miss Vara was a very pretty girl.

"What is she, Spanish? Mexican?"

"No—I mean, I guess she could be," Bugs said. Because he wasn't ashamed, naturally, and of course she'd probably find out the truth from Ford, sooner or later. But right now he wasn't up to explaining why he'd been in Westex with a Negro maid.

"She's very pretty." Amy repeated. "If you like that type. She doesn't strike me as someone who'd wear very well, but I'm probably mistaken. I hope she isn't in any trouble?"

"She isn't. Your friend Ford was just throwing his weight around."

"That isn't like Lou." Amy shook her head serenely. "Perhaps he didn't go about it in the right way, but I'm sure that he must have had a good reason to—"

"And I'm sure he didn't have! What were you doing over there today, anyhow? I mean"—Bugs got a grip on his temper—"it's your own business. You don't owe me any explanations. But—"

"Why, I don't mind," said Amy; and she didn't seem to. On the contrary. "Lou goes to Westex quite frequently. I don't know why exactly, but it's the largest city in the county, so I suppose there'd be any number of reasons why he might have to. I rode over with him to see about finding a job."

"Then it was just a coincidence that we bumped into each other?" Bugs said disbelievingly. "He wasn't—*huh?* You went to see about a job?"

"Yes. The schoolboard discharged me yesterday. That's why I was so upset when you came to the house last night."

"But why did—" he caught himself. "I guess you'd probably rather not talk about it."

"I don't mind, now. I was pretty torn up about it at the time, but now that it's happened . . . It was because of that day I was at Lou's house. You know. The afternoon that y-you—that you came there. Someone saw me going out the back door, and the word got around. And yesterday I was fired."

"I see," Bugs mumbled. "Uh—did you get the job today?"

"No. I think Lou took steps to see that I wouldn't get it. In fact, I think he may have had quite a bit to do with my losing my teacher's job." She looked at him, smiling at his expression. "No, I'm not angry about it. I was, and I probably will be again. But I always know that Lou thinks a great deal of me. If he does something like this—well, it's meant for my own good."

Bugs's eyes narrowed angrily, but he didn't say anything. He didn't trust himself to. Ford had compromised her. He'd helped to get her canned from one job, and he'd kept her from getting another one. And he was fully prepared, apparently, to continue with the same hateful line of conduct. Yet she sat here defending him. Saying he did these things for her own good!

"You see," she went on, "Lou feels that his own life is wasted. He hates what he's doing. He's not suited to it, and it's twisted him. Actually, he's very scholarly. He was a brilliant student, and—"

"*Him?* Ford?"

"It's hard to believe, isn't it?" Amy nodded. "But, yes, Lou's very brilliant. He graduated from high school when he was fifteen. He went through pre-med in three years. Then, in his first year of medical college, his father took very ill and Lou came home. Doctor Ford—his father, that is—didn't get any worse, but he didn't get any better either. He just lingered on, year after year. And Lou . . ."

Ford had felt that he had to stay with the old man. But there was nothing in the small town for him to do. No suitable work, no real challenge for his mind. Still, he had to do something, and because he was "old family" he had been given a deputy sheriff's appointment. It was no job for a book-learned dude, obviously. For a man with ambitions which would be interpreted as pretensions. You had to blend with those around you, with the public's conception of a cowtown deputy. So Ford had blended. He had fitted himself into the role with a vengeance, exaggerating it until it bordered on caricature. And with this outward twisting of the man, there had been an inward one. In the brain—the intelligence—which could not be used as it had been intended to be.

". . . very high-handed and arrogant," Amy was saying. "He won't explain himself. If you can't see things as clearly as he does, then it's your own fault. You'd better smarten-up, as he'd put it. But he'll do a great deal for someone he really likes, and what he does is usually right."

Bugs gritted his teeth. It was all he could do to control himself. Finally, his voice merely sarcastic, he asked just what great plans Ford had in mind for her.

"Well," Amy said, thoughtful. "I believe he originally intended to make me leave town. To force me out into the world. Now, I think he's decided that I may belong here, so . . ." she broke off, blushing for some reason. "Why don't we change the subject, hmm? It's hard for me to understand Lou, and I know it must be a lot harder for you."

Bugs let the statement pass, but he *did* understand Ford—to his own way of thinking. He had Ford figured right down to a tee. He hadn't reached his conclusions hastily. On the contrary, he'd been willing, even anxious, to believe that the deputy was okay. But Ford's own actions, one piled upon another, had made any such belief impossible.

He was convinced of Ford's unalloyed, unrelieved black-ness, because Ford himself had so convinced him.

That was that. It was maddeningly aggravating that Amy couldn't see the truth about the man.

. . .It was about ten o'clock on the night of his return from Westex. Dozing uneasily, almost as much awake as asleep, Bugs heard a faint sound at his door.

He sat up, started to jump up. Then, he quietly lay down again. Listening. Watching with slitted eyes.

There was a *click*; a faint draft of air and flash of light, as the door opened and closed. Silence for a moment. An almost-silence. Then a rustling sound, a series of rustles, protracted over several seconds. And then stealthy foot-steps.

They traversed the brief areaway past the bathroom. They stopped, right at his bedside.

Bugs couldn't actually see the intruder; only that there was one. Only a blurred shadow among the darker shadows of the room. But that was enough.

He moved suddenly, moving with that incredible swiftness of which very big men are sometimes capable. His arms swept out and swept shut. His body rose and came down again, pinning the intruder beneath him.

"Now, by God!" he grunted savagely. "Just what the—"

The sentence ended in a startled gulp. He had reacted rather than acted, his movements rushing ahead of his thoughts. But now—

The body squirmed delicately. Making certain adjustments. Fitting him into its bared flesh, its soft, warm, gently undulant contours.

Then, there was a contented sigh. And a delicious shudder of anticipation. And a tense, almost desperate whisper:

"You're not angry, Mr. McKenna? Y-You think less of m-me, Mr. McKenna? I've wanted to so long, and . . ."

"Rosie," said Bugs.

And that was all he said. That either of them said. For quite a while.

He had gotten to bed about five after his return from Westex. Very tired, but with too much on his mind for sleep. With a riddle which had to be solved, yet was seemingly unsolvable. For Rosalie Vara was out of the blackmail picture now—and he was very glad of it. But if she was out, then who was in?

In actuality, she had been his only suspect. There had been two possibles—she and Joyce Hanlon—but Joyce had been in her suite at the time of Dudley's death. So it had to be Rosalie. It had had to be something that wasn't and couldn't be. She was in the clear and Joyce was in the clear. The only two women who, by any stretch of the imagination, could have been in Dudley's room, or, rather, his bath room.

The only two women . . .

Well, couldn't it possibly have been a man? It *could* have been, couldn't it? After all, there was someone and if it wasn't a woman, then it had to be a man. That makes sense, doesn't it, McKenna?

Bugs supposed that it did. But he also knew no man was involved in the matter.

Dudley had been staging a little party there in his bathroom. A sex party. And in the intimacy of their secret carousing, his guest had slipped him a mickey.

He wouldn't have had a man in his bath. What would have been the point in that? Why would a man want to keep secret the presence of another man?

Then there was that mickey—the choloral hydrate. As Ford had pointed out, it was traditionally a woman's weapon. A man might clout you or mug you, or stick a gun in your ribs. A woman did the job with chloral. She couldn't muscle you, so she honeyed up to you. She got your guard down, got you to thinking about things that weren't discussed in Sunday school. Got you to the point where you weren't thinking at all—just wanting—and then she gave you a drink. And right after that the party suddenly ended. You were in the land of bye-bye. And if you'd gotten a big enough dose, you might not ever emerge from it.

So it had to be a woman, which meant that it couldn't be a man. But since it couldn't be a woman either—despite its having to be, why—well, where were you for God's sake?

Bugs was acquiring a violent headache. Also, at long last, he was beginning to get drowsy.

Now, who . . . what . . . he thought. Not a man or a woman. Not a man . . . or a woman. Not someone you'd think of as being . . .

He almost had it. The only logical answer. He thought the seeming paradox through, was on the verge of the exceedingly simple explanation. And, then, at that very moment, he'd fallen asleep.

And when he awakened he had other things to think about.

. . . She came back from the bathroom, bringing him a drink from the ice-water tap. She sat down on the edge of the bed, a little shy now, timid, and pulled a corner of the sheet over her naked thighs. Bugs had been about to make a suggestion: that she should address him less formally in view of what had transpired between them. Now, he decided that he wouldn't. She was a funny kid. Apparently, she was more comfortable mister-ing him, yet she might take his suggestion as an order.

Out in the oil fields somewhere, there was a sudden mass of light. Not a flash but a mass, racing and spreading through the darkness, so brilliant and far-extended that some of its glare came down into the court of the Hanlon, and filtered around the drapes at Bugs's windows. There was the light; then, since sound, of course, travels much more slowly than light, a thunderous explosion. It came from at least a mile away, Bugs estimated, but the blast rattled the Hanlon's windows.

Rosalie shivered and gripped Bugs's hand. He squeezed it reassuringly. "A big one, huh? Must have been a battery of boilers going up."

"Oh, how terrible! Do you suppose anyone was hurt?"

"Naw, sure not," he lied, touched by her concern. "Look Rosie, I—Is it okay for you to come on duty so early? It won't get you in trouble?"

It wasn't the question he'd started to ask. He'd checked himself out of regard for her. Because in telling him what he really wanted to know—as she probably would have out of loyalty and affection—she *could* get into trouble.

"No" —she shook her head to the query. "As long as I put in a full shift, and get my work done, I can come early or late. Within reason, of course."

"Uh-huh. Well, that's good," he said.

Drifting in on the night breeze now was a wailing, eerie chorus of sirens. Ambulances were speeding out from the emergency hospitals—as numerous in the oil fields as drinkstands at a carnival—to the scene of the disaster. The sound dwindled and was lost in the distance. Rosalie freed the hand that Bugs was holding and got up.

She had left her clothes in the areaway. Bringing them back to the bed, she sat down again and began to dress. Bugs made a movement to help her. Shyly, she drew away a little.

"I want to tell you something, Mr. McKenna. Two things. First—I won't do anything like this again. I'm glad it happened. I wanted to—wanted you to have me. You stood up for me against Mr. Ford, and I can't tell you how grateful I am. And—"

"I don't want you to be, Rosie. I don't want you to feel that you owe me anything."

"I know. You wouldn't want me to." Her soft voice trembled with emotion. "But, anyway. What I started to say, Mr. McKenna, was that—that—"

This was both the beginning and the end of their affair she said in effect. It would have to be, obviously, since its continuation was certain to bring tragedy and trouble.

Bugs protested—he felt that he had to—but he was deeply relieved. He wasn't in love with her, nor she with him. And a thing like this, life being as it was, could only drag them both downhill. As the Hanlon's house detective, the official paid to nip potential trouble in the bud, he was in a far better position to avoid discovery than most; than, say, Dudley had been—one of the watched, rather than the watchman. Yet discovery was virtually inevitable, in the long run; and he was in enough of a mess now without taking on another.

Hell, if he could just get out of this present mess; get out of it, and get to feeling right about Amy, or stop feeling anything about her. Either accept what had happened between her and Ford, or—

"There was something else I wanted to tell you, Mr. McKenna. About Mr. Ford. He—"

"Don't," Bugs said. "I don't think you'd better."

"I'm going to," Rosalie said firmly. "He doesn't really suspect me. Probably you guessed that. But that's only part of it. The real reason he wanted to talk to me—"

Bugs cut her off. "Didn't he warn you not to tell me, Rosie? Well, then, let me say it. He figures that there must have been two people, a man and a woman, with Dudley. The woman gave him the chloral, and the man knock—pushed him out the window. And he's got me figured as the man."

"Yes, sir. And it's so crazy, Mr. McKenna! I mean, why would you—why would anyone do it? If the woman had already killed him, as good as killed him, why—"

"That misunderstanding we had at the post office today," Bugs said. "I imagine Ford asked you about that? No, don't tell me—"

"Of course, I'll tell you! Yes, he did ask me, and—and I didn't know quite what to say, Mr. McKenna. I didn't understand it myself, and I was afraid if I tried to lie to him—"

"I'm glad you didn't. You did the right thing, just telling him what happened and letting it go at that. But . . . but that's the set-up, Rosie. It's a pretty weak thread, but he wants to stick me, and he's trying to use that little frammis at the post office to do it."

"But I . . . I don't see how that . . ."

"Well," Bugs said cautiously, "it's really pretty simple. I'm just guessing, of course; I don't actually know. But it seems to me that Ford's thinking would just have to run like this: The man doesn't know that the woman is in Dudley's room. Perhaps she's in the bathroom, see? But she knows that he's in there—and knows who he is—and when he apparently kills Dudley, and takes the money she came there to steal, why . . ."

He left the sentence unfinished. He could see something of her now, his eyes having adjusted to the darkness, and the expression on her face stopped him.

"I see," she said, at last. "You thought I was the woman with Dudley. You thought I was trying to blackmail you, and you tried to—"

"No! I didn't really think it, Rosie! I was just desperate, snatching at straws, you know, and—"

"It's all right, Mr. McKenna," she said gently. "I understand. Believe me, when you're what I am, when you've lived as I have, you get a lot of understanding. All that matters is that you don't think that about me now."

"I don't. I never did."

"I'm glad . . . Were you getting up now, Mr. McKenna? I'm doing a room on the floor below, and if you are getting up . . ."

"Sure, save you another trip," Bugs said. "About that time, anyway."

"I'll run along, then. 'Bye, now."

'Bye, now. Good-bye, period, to anything more than friendly politeness. Bugs dressed and left the room, wondering why things had to be the way they were. Reluctantly relieved that they were that way.

He ate.

He made his tour of the corridors, and started his back-o'-the-house inspection. Except for the kitchens, it was generally inactive, its various entrances and exits closed and locked at this hour. It was part of Bugs's duties to unlock them and have a look around. Making sure that no sneak-thief had wangled his way inside, watchful against the ever-present danger of fire.

Bakery, laundry, grocery. Printers', painters', electricians', plumbers' and carpenters' shops. Ice plant and ice-cream plant. Rug reweaving, upholstering, linen repair. Boiler-room, engine-room, waterworks . . . The hotel was a city, and it contained everything necessary for the operation of a city.

Twice during his tour, Bugs encountered Leslie Eaton, once the clerk was hustling toward the valet department, the second time as he was leaving the telephone-switchboard room. He was carrying a batch of charge slips on every occasion. So, ostensibly, he was in pursuit of his duties. But Bugs guessed that he did a hell of a lot of chasing around that wasn't necessary. Westbrook had always thought so; and Eaton seemed to be absent from the front office about as much as he was there.

The clerk smirked and blushed as they passed. Frowning, Bugs looked after him from the door of the telephone room.

Now, what was there about that guy, anyway? What possible connection could there be between Eaton and the jam he was in?

Not a thing that he could think of, although there was a troubled stirring in the deep recesses of his mind. Bugs shrugged, and went on through the door.

It was a three-position board, but only one operator was on duty now. Bugs sat down next to her on one of the long-legged swivel chairs, chatting idly with her between calls, watching the nimbly casual movement of her fingers.

It was interesting. Everything about the hotel was interesting to him. Often since he had come here, he had looked back into the past, compared its drabness and dullness and sameness with the ever-changing, always-intriguing world of the hotel. And he had shuddered over what he had escaped from, felt the deepest gratitude for what he had escaped into.

He never wanted to leave here. It would be nice, of course, if he could rise to a better job, but if he couldn't . . . well, he wouldn't kick. Just staying on here would be enough.

And he was going to do it! He wasn't going to take another rap. He wasn't going to take it on the lam. He was going to stay. Somehow, somehow. Regardless of the price for staying.

He'd shot square with people all his life, and it hadn't got him anywhere. Now, if shooting square wouldn't do the job, he'd get it done the other way.

The operator glanced at the clock. Propping her morning call-sheets in front of her, she pushed a plug into the board: "Good morning, sir. It's six o'clock . . ."

Bugs left. He went down to and through the lobby, strolled around the block, and entered the coffee shop.

He had breakfast, read the morning paper. By then it was eight o'clock, the end of his shift, and he started for his room.

He heard his name called. He turned and waited as Lou Ford came up the steps from the side entrance.

"Well?" he said.

"You're in trouble," Ford said. "Let's talk about it."

They went to Bugs's room. Ford settled himself into the one easy chair, lighted one of his thin black cigars, and spewed out a fragrant cloud of smoke. He fanned it with one hand, staring at Bugs with absent thoughtfulness. Bugs stared back at him stolidly.

There was something different about the deputy today, but he couldn't quite put his finger on it. Then Ford spoke again, and he realized what it was.

Ford's drawl was gone; his errors and exaggerations of speech. He spoke as any literate person might have.

"I said you were in trouble, Bugs. That may have been putting it a little strong. I might be more accurate to say that you're on the verge of trouble, but that you can avoid it. I can help you to."

"I see."

"I hope so, but I doubt it. Perhaps we'd better let that lie a moment, and go back to the beginning. Back to the day when I took you out of jail and got you your job here." He took another puff from his cigar, tapped the ash into the wastebasket. "Incidentally, I gather that you like it here. You wouldn't mind sticking around permanently."

"That's right."

"I'd like to have you stick around."

Bugs shrugged, waited silently. There was a faint flicker in Ford's eyes, a hint of annoyance which might readily become something else. But he went on level-voiced.

"Well, as I said, perhaps we'd better go back to the beginning. I don't like to. It's not my way to do favors for people and then throw it up to them. Or even to let them know I'm doing them a favor. But in this case . . . You came here with nothing, Bugs. Nothing but a bad record. I got you out of jail. I staked you. I got you linked up with this job. I introduced you to—"

"Better stop there. Leave her out of it."

"All right. We'll stop with the other things I did. You were sore at the world, about as touchy as a man can get. So I tried not to make you feel that you were being favored. I did what I did in a way that you could accept, so that you could possibly feel that you were favoring me. I told you that this place needed a good two-fisted house dick. It would save me and my boys work if you'd take the job."

He paused, puffing at his cigar again. Bugs yawned, making no very great effort to stifle it.

"Maybe you'd better get to the point," he said. "You gave me the world with a ring around it. Now, you want something in return. All right, I don't expect something for nothing. What is it you want."

"Not as much as I gave, Bugs. Not nearly as much. I was established here; I had a lot to lose if I was wrong about you. And judging by your record, I could easily have been wrong. But I took you on trust. Now, I'd like some of that trust back."

"That still doesn't tell me anything. You still—"

"Doesn't tell you anything! Now, goddammit—" Ford's mouth snapped shut. After a moment he went on again. Drawling a little, gradually slipping back into his usual manner of speech. "Let's get to that trouble we was talkin' about. Cut around the frills and get right to the heart of it. You went to Dudley's room for some reason. You scuffled with him, and he got knocked out the window. Now—"

"Uh-uh. I've got an alibi for the time of his death."

"You have, huh? An' what time would that be?"

"Well—uh—what I mean is," Bugs said, "that I've got all my time covered. I went straight from my room to the elevator, and I didn't go upstairs after that until . . ."

"You went straight from your room to the elevator, sure. An' you sure went to a hell of a lot of trouble to be able to prove it. But you got no way of provin' that you didn't leave your room before that. Or"—Ford cocked an eyebrow at him—"have you? You prove it to me, if you can, an' me, I'll vamoose right out of here."

"I don't have to prove it."

"I wouldn't lay no bets on that. No, sir, I sure wouldn't, and that's a fact."

"Now, look," Bugs said doggedly. "Why tab me with this thing, anyway? The fact that there was a man in Dudley's room—if there was one—doesn't necessarily mean that it was me. You've got no—"

"Let's talk about what it does necessarily mean. The guy didn't break in. He didn't sneak in, like with a passkey maybe. A sneak would've just copped and cleared out. He wouldn't've been scufflin' with Dudley, or—"

"He would if Dudley had caught him."

"Which"—Ford winked—"Dudley was havin' too much fun to do. Howsome-ever, suppose he did. The guy'd have no right to be there. No matter how no-account Dudley was, he'd've put up a racket about it, let out a yell or called for help. An' we know he didn't do that. Then there's that gal in the bathroom—the one we both know was there. In a case like we're supposin' about, I don't see her livin' but a mite longer than Dudley did. Because this fella'd be a pro. He wouldn't leave nothin' behind that was worth takin', or nothin' that'd put the finger on him. So, he'd check that bathroom just as sure as God made green apples. An' that'd been the end of the gal."

Ford leaned back in his chair, crossed one booted foot over the other. Bugs glowered at him helplessly, wanting nothing so much as to smash his fist into the deputy's bland, saturnine face.

"Ain't hard to figure out at all, is it?" Ford said. "No, sir, they's prob'ly plenty of four-year-old boys that could do it without turnin' a hair. Dudley let this fella into his room. The guy was someone in authority, an' he had to. Who had that much authority—enough to make a man open up his room late at night? Not more'n two people that I can think of. One of 'em was Westbrook, an'—"

"Forget him!" Bugs said curtly. "Westbrook couldn't have had anything to do with it."

Ford nodded. His tone decidedly less edged. "Glad you said that, Bugs. A man that'll stick up for a friend when it hurts has got plenty to him. But o' course you're right. The first thing I done was to check on Westbrook, an' I know he wouldn't've been callin' on Dudley. His hands were tied. He'd insisted that Dudley was absolutely okay, so he couldn't . . . But they's no use goin' into that, is there? Or into the set-to of ours over in Westex."

"What is there use in going into?"

"What happened, Bugs? Did Westbrook ask you to help him out with Dudley? Try to get the money back for him?"

"No! Well, all right, he did ask me. But I refused."

"Uh-huh, sure. Just couldn't take a chance on gettin' into trouble." Ford drew on his cigar, exhaled a thin stream of smoke. "And then you changed your mind. An' this trouble you was afraid of happened."

Bugs shrugged. Ford could talk, theorize, until he was blue in the face. But he couldn't prove anything.

The deputy studied him narrow-eyed, spoke as though in rebuttal to a statement.

"Not yet," he said. "But I ain't tried real hard. Ain't really put my mind to it. Ain't decided whether I want to do any provin'. If I do . . ."

"Then you'll have to do some proving against someone else. The woman who gave Dudley the chloral."

"Why?"

"Why?" Bugs frowned. "Why, dammit, because you will!

You can't—couldn't—"

"Why not? What's to stop me?" Ford spread his hands. Maybe they was a mistake about the chloral. Maybe the gal just saw you comin' out of Dudley's room, and wasn't actually there herself."

"But—but she was there! You've said so a dozen times!"

"Could be I was wrong. Might say somethin' else the thirteenth time. Wouldn't be too unreasonable, y'know. If she was willin' to stand right up and be counted—to do her duty, irregardless, like an upstandin' citizen should—why, a fella'd just about have to figure she was on the level. Yes, sir, it wouldn't be no bother for him at all—even if it wasn't sort o' handy for him to figure that way."

"And even if he wasn't in a position where he could call his shots any way he wanted to."

"Now, you're gettin' the idea," Ford beamed. "Really smartenin' up now. You keep on an' you'll be able to pour sand out of a boot without a book of directions."

Then, he laughed pleasantly, infectiously, stroked his jaw with a slender-fingered hand.

"Now, listen to me, will you? Been carryin' on that way so long that I can't stop even when I want to. Just slide into it without thinkin'. But we all got our little peculiarities, usually got good reasons for 'em, too, the way I see it. And as long as a man don't fault the other fella for his—"

"Look," Bugs cut in. "If you've got something to say—"

"Sure. You're tired, and I ain't exactly the soothingest man in the world to talk to. So we'll wind it up fast. I can't see you as deliberately tyin' into Dudley, not for money or anything else. Aside from that—and maybe I got kind of a funny outlook on these things—I figure there wasn't nothing lost when he died. Just saved the law a job it'd have to do sooner or later. So you tell me it was an accident, and I'll believe you. Won't be nothin' more said or done about it."

"Yeah? Well, I'm not telling you that!"

"Well—" Ford hesitated, his lips pursed thoughtfully. "Well, okay. We'll still skip it. I gave you a lot of trust in the beginning, and I'll give you that much more. And, now, Bugs"—he lowered his voice, leaned forward in his chair—"I want a dividend on that trust. You know what's building up here. You know why Mrs. Hanlon was so helpful in getting you a job; you'd just about have to by this time. All right, take it from there. What have you got to say about it?"

He leaned back in his chair again. Bugs squirmed fretfully. He was over a barrel. What was he supposed to say that would take him off of it?

"Listen," he began. "What . . . I mean, dammit, what do you—"

"I can't tell you that. If I had to, it wouldn't mean anything. Wouldn't know for sure whether it jibed with what you had in mind. And if it didn't, I'd be behind the eight ball. I'd fluff somethin' that just better not be fluffed."

"But, hell . . ."

"I'm already way out on a limb, Bugs. A lot further than even a real trustin' fella ought to go. I've saddled a hoss for you an' given you a hand-up, and all I'm doin' now is grippin' the bridle. Just holdin' a little in my finger tips, until I see which way you're headin'."

"And if it isn't the way you're heading, I get set down hard?"

"If you're that dumb, yeah. Me, I got an awful low boilin' point for dumbness. Riles me worse'n a cactus under a saddle blanket."

"But what—"

But there was no use asking that again. Ford, in a way, occupied the same position Bugs was in.

Did he want Mike Hanlon killed?—Bugs's cooperation in murdering the old man? Possibly, in fact, very probably, it would seem. But Ford couldn't say so until he was sure of Bugs's feelings.

Or did he want the opposite? To pin a rap of conspiracy of attempt to commit murder on Joyce Hanlon? That also was possible. But again Ford could not admit it without knowing Bugs's sentiments. Bugs might tip off Joyce. Forewarned, she would hold her plans in abeyance, and Hanlon would never be safe.

"Well?" Ford said. "Well, Bugs?"

"I don't know what you're talking 'bout," Bugs said. "I don't know and I don't want to know."

Ford took the cigar from his mouth, studied the tip of it absently. He rolled it between his fingers, then let it drop into the wastebasket.

"So you don't know," he said. "Ain't got the slightest idea of what I been talkin' about. Could be that that's an answer itself, which ain't to say, of course, that I'm real fond of it."

"Look, Ford," Bugs said. "Honest to God, now, don't you think you're asking a hell of a lot?"

"Well, maybe," Ford nodded judiciously. "Yes, sir, I could be. Wouldn't be too much to ask of a man, but seein' that you're more in the nature of a man with a boy's head . . ."

"Go on," Bugs grunted. "You know I have to take it."

"Ain't it the truth? Yes, sir, it's plain gospel an that's a fact . . ."

Ford continued to talk. For a full five minutes, the bitter, biting drawl lashed Bugs unmercifully, leaving him sick and shaking with fear and fury. Then, at last, it was over, and the deputy stood up.

"Been meanin' to tell you that for a long time," he said mildly. "Just by way of bein' helpful, y' know. It ain't got no direct bearin' on the problem we been discussin'. About that now—that no-answer answer you gave me—I guess we'll just have to wait an' see. Or maybe it'd be better to say I'll wait and see. I'll do the waitin' and seein', and you can be doin' some real hard hopin'."

Bugs ate dinner at Amy's house that night. It was a simple but tasty meal of baked beans, salad and cornbread. But you couldn't have proved it by him. As absorbed in worry as he was, he could have eaten sawdust and brickbats and never known the difference.

A full stomach stilled the worries to an extent. Replaced them with an uneasy sluggishness. He helped her wash and dry the dishes, and then they moved into the livingroom. They talked, seated on the ancient horsehair sofa, with Bugs's contributions to the converstion growing fewer and fewer, shorter and shorter. Finally, he lapsed into a complete and prolonged silence.

Amy nudged him. She got up suddenly, sat down on his knees, and kissed him on the mouth. Now, she said, would he wake up? Would he or not wake up? Bugs woke up. Even in his black mood, the treatment was effective. Amy allowed him to demonstrate that he was fully awake. Then, pulling away a little, she tilted his chin up with her hand.

"Mac . . . what's bothering you? I'm sure something must be."

"Naw," Bugs shrugged. "Just dopey, is all. Didn't sleep too good today." Then he shifted his eyes, added casually, "What have I got to be bothered about?"

"I don't know. Would you tell me if you were in—if you were having trouble of any kind?"

"Well, sure. Why not? If I thought you wanted to hear about it."

"You wouldn't be . . . you wouldn't think that you couldn't trust me?"

Bugs kissed her. He couldn't or wouldn't answer the question in his own mind, so he did it that way. Amy seemed satisfied, and dropped the subject.

But the following night, as he was leaving, she brought it up again.

"I'm not asking what the trouble is, Mac. Just if there is any."

"Now, listen, Amy—"

"I'm sorry. I just thought that might be the reason, you know. Why you didn't say anything to me about . . . anything. I mean, if you were in trouble you might feel that— Oh, just listen to me!" She laughed suddenly, with brittle shrillness. "Did you ever hear anyone so mixed-up in your life?"

"Amy . . ." Bugs began.

"No. No, please, Mac!" She stepped back through the door, leaving him on the porch. "I'm tired and it's getting late, and—You run along, now, and I'll see you tomorrow night."

The door closed, the lock clicked, the hall light went off. Bugs turned uncertainly and headed for the hotel.

It was still short of ten-thirty when he reached the Hanlon. Plenty of time yet before he was due on the job. He parked his car at the side of the building and remained in it.

Smoking and brooding. Watching the street ahead of him.

The more he thought about it, the more chagrined he became over his trip to Westex City. He'd really pinned a label on himself with that stunt. Tied a rope around his neck and handed the other end to Lou Ford. And, hell, even if he hadn't run into Ford, or if Ford hadn't been tailing him, the trip still would have been so much time wasted.

He couldn't hang around the Westex general-delivery window. He couldn't hang around indefinitely outside the building. Rather, he could, but what the hell could he expect it to make him? Because, naturally, as any damned fool should know, the blackmailer wasn't going to go near the place. There'd be a third party, someone Bugs wouldn't know or recognize. And why, in the name of God, he hadn't seen that—!

Well—Bugs grudgingly excused himself—there'd been no apparent necessity for him to think of it. He'd been sure that the blackmailer was Rosalie Vara—equally confident that she was sufficiently naive to walk into his trap. He'd've known better, of course, if he'd known that the woman in question was a mickey artist. But he'd had no way of knowing that. So he'd done what he had, and it wasn't particularly stupid under the circumstances. And, anyway, there was no use in beating himself over the head about it now.

The point was that the traditional trap for a blackmailer—the only one he could think of—would not work in this case. Not for a man who was on the wrong side of the fence himself and could get no aid from the other side. Somehow, he'd just have to figure out who she was—*if* it was a she. And he already knew that it wasn't, that it couldn't be, and he also knew that—

Savagely, Bugs hurled his cigarette out the window, severed the nagging circle of his thoughts.

Similarly, he refused to think about what he would do when, and if, he caught up with-him-her-it—whoever the blackmailer was. He'd do *something*, that was a cinch. Whatever was necessary. Couldn't say what it would be until the time came.

A bellboy was crossing the intersection at the next corner.

A slick-haired youth, with a pale phlegmatic face. A cigarette dangled from the corner of his mouth, and he carried a canvas mailsack over his shoulder.

He came down the walk with the tiredly jaunty stride peculiar to bellboys. Nearing the side entrance, he took a long pull on the cigarette, flicked it into the street. And went through the double doors at what was practically a trot. Bugs grinned sourly to himself. Those damned bellboys; they worked *at* a hotel, rather than for it. The hotel was only one of numerous bosses, the people they waited on: the cranks and drunks, the grouches and snides, the rubes and the sharpies. And to survive they learned every trick in the book. They had to be pulling some kind of swiftie—no matter how small—or they just didn't feel right.

This lad now, he'd probably dogged it all the way to the post office and back. But, returning, he went through the door like he was shot out of a gun.

Bugs smoked another cigarette. Then he got out of the car and moved slowly toward the side door. The mail the bellboy had brought would be the last one until tomorrow. It was a light mail, due to the lateness of the pick-up, so it should be all put up in the room-boxes by now. He could find out now whether—

He didn't want to. If there was a letter, well, there'd be a letter. But there was no point in running to look for a headache.

He walked around to the front of the Hanlon and entered the coffee shop. He had coffee and some cherry pie à la mode, and went through the doors to the lobby.

Feet dragging unconsciously, he came down the marble checkerboard of its floor to the front office. He stopped parallel with the key rack, turned and looked.

There wasn't any letter. Only another call-slip from Joyce Hanlon. He accepted it with a suppressed sigh of relief and began his tour of the corridors.

Probably, he decided, he ought to give Joyce a ring sometime soon. After all, she might want to talk to him about something other than what he had assumed she did. And, anyhow, there could be no harm in just talking. It could be, even, that he'd be doing himself a favor. Might find out something from her that would be useful to know. As, for example, just how things stood between her and Lou Ford.

Yeah, he guessed he'd better do it. Every reason why he should, and none—practically—why he shouldn't.

By two in the morning, he had completed his rounds of the room floors. He had also worked up enough appetite to want a square meal. He got off the elevator and started for the coffee shop. And, then, as he was passing the front office—the key-rack section—he came to a dead stop.

He stared, incredulously.

He moved slowly up to the counter.

Leslie Eaton was gone, and Ted Gusick was tending desk. He reached the letter out of Bugs's box and handed it to him. Bugs looked at the pencil-addressed envelope, at the faint Westex City postmark. He stood tapping it on the counter, dully. Wondering what—how—why—

Wondering.

There'd been no mail since that last one, the one that he'd seen the day bellboy bring in. If this letter had been in that mail, it should have been put in his box hours ago.

Slowly, Bugs raised his eyes, looked into the smooth poker-face of Ted Gusick.

"Something wrong, Mr. McKenna? Any little thing I can do for you?"

"What?" Bugs blinked, "Oh, no. No, everything's swell. I was just wondering—uh—well, where Eaton was. Nothing that can't wait, but—"

"Well, I've got three bells that can't wait much longer. One of the parties has already called down a second time."

"Uh-huh. Yeah, sure," Bugs murmured vaguely.

"Understand there's a new night engineer. Big muscle man, y'know. Maybe he's got our blushing boy bent over a boiler."

He laughed, winked. Then, misreading Bugs's startled scowl, he retreated swiftly into his usual suavely reserved self. "Not a very good joke was it, Mr. McKenna, sir? Of course, I couldn't really think that about a fine young man like Mr. Eaton."

Think it? Hell, it was something you'd know if you knew anything at all! It stuck out all over the guy. And . . . and it must be the answer to the puzzle. It hadn't been a woman in Dudley's bathroom. Not a woman literally, but—

"Now, that I think of it," Ted continued. "I believe you might find Mr. Eaton down in the valet shop. He had some charges to check there, and he probably stopped to get a free pants-press."

"Pants . . . pressed?" Bugs said, not knowing what he said. Or that he said anything. "Pants pressed?"

"Excuse me—*ha, ha*— I honestly didn't mean that as another joke, Mr. McKenna. But, yes, sir"—Ted nodded seriously. "The valet's always glad to do those things if he isn't busy, so Mr. Eaton could be getting his p—suit pressed."

Bugs turned abruptly and walked away. In the alcove leading to the coffee shop, he paused and took the letter from his pocket.

He hadn't really taken a good look at the first one, its envelope rather. Still, unnoticing he had noticed; certain things about it had registered on his subconscious. And repeated on this envelope, they soared to the surface of his mind, attained glaring significance.

He ran his fingers over the paper where the address was inscribed. He studied the almost indiscernible date of the postmark. Grimly, then, he went on into the coffee shop, returning the letter unopened to his pocket.

Never mind what the thing said. The guy who had said it—written it—was what he was interested in.

He sat down on a stool near one end of the horseshoe counter and gave his order to a waitress. Then, with a grunt of dismay, he hastily got up. "Just remembered a phone call I got to make. Hold that order a few minutes, will you?"

The girl smiled and said she would. Bugs laid his hat on his stool, squeezed through the service slot between counter and wall, and moved swiftly toward the rear of the coffee shop. Back of the coffee shop was the hotel's main kitchen. Bugs entered it through another service slot and hurried down its vast, dimly lit length. It was not in use at this hour, since the dining-room, which it served, was closed. Bugs left it by a door at its far end and emerged onto the back landing.

The out-of-use service elevator was parked there. He entered it, cut off the lights, and piloted it down to the first basement. Quietly, he eased the door open, stood listening in the darkness.

The valet shop was about twenty feet to his right. Eaton's voice drifted down the corridor to him:

"Oh, don't be so nasty! I guess I had to check these charges, didn't I?"

"Charges? Goddammit, you been here long enough to check Fort Knox!"

Eaton emitted a high-pitched giggle. Bugs squirmed nervously. As busy as the coffee shop was, time would go very quickly for that waitress. He could stay away twenty or thirty minutes and it would seem like only a "few" to her. Longer than that, however, he'd be putting a dangerous strain on his alibi. And at the rate this damned silly Eaton was stalling . . . !

"I AM going, darn it! I said I was, and I am. How many times do I have to tell you?"

"None, by God! Just show me! Just get the hell out, so I can get some work done!"

Eaton made a pouting sound. The gate to the railed-off valet shop clicked open; swung creaking, to and fro, as his footsteps came hurriedly down the corridor.

Bugs tensed. His hand shot out, suddenly, grasping Eaton, yanking him into the car, flinging him with breathtaking impact against its rear wall. Then, almost before the door had closed, he shot the elevator upward.

Between the seventh and eighth floors, he brought the car to a stop. He switched on the lights, and turned slowly around.

Eaton met his gaze, smirking. He was still a little startled, but apparently not at all frightened. His seeming cocksureness infuriated Bugs.

"All right, buster," he growled. "Start talking!"

"Talking?" The clerk tittered nervously. "Juth—just about anything, Mr. McKenna?"

"Don't pull that crap on me! You try crapping me, and I'll scramble every goddamned cell in your skull!"

"B-but Mr. McKenna"—Eaton's smirk had frozen. "Mr. McKenna, I juth d-don't—"

"You think I'm stupid? You think I wouldn't ever see through a deal like that? Two weeks ago—about two weeks— you went over to Westex City. You mailed some letters addressed in pencil to yourself back here. Then, you erased your address and readdressed them to me. And—"

"But I didn't! W-what—why would I do that?"

"To give yourself an alibi, damn you! I'd get a letter, but you wouldn't have been in Westex the day before—the day it would ordinarily have been mailed to me. Might have got away with it, too, if you'd done a little more erasing on these postmarks. Well"—Bugs took him by the lapels— "that's it. Now—"

"Mr. McKenna," Eaton said evenly. "Why would I write you a letter? What would I write you about?"

"You know what about! You were there in the r—" Bugs stopped abruptly. Eaton might not be positive of his information. Mustn't say anything that would corroborate what he had. "I know those letters didn't come in on the regular mail. Not the one I got tonight, at least. So—"

"The first one didn't either, Mr. McKenna. I mean, I know it didn't now. That's why I—why I got to wondering about them."

"Go on. Keep talking, and make it good."

"I found it lying down on the floor between the counter and the room-boxes. I thought at the time that it must have fallen out of the box, so I just dusted it off and put it back in. But"—the clerk's eyes fell, and his voice went very low—"but-but you never get any letters, and, well, I'm— I've always been interested in anything that concerns you. So I did notice the date. I saw that it had been postmarked two days before, a day before that day it should have been. And, well, that made me more curious, and—"

"Spill it out," Bugs said gruffly, unaccountably embarrassed. "Come on!"

"Mr. McKenna . . . I guess you haven't opened the second letter have you? If you had, you'd know that I wouldn't, uh—" He broke off hurriedly, timidly. "Well, anyway, I found the second letter right where I'd found the first. On the floor, between the counter and the room-box

rack. And it had the same date as the first one. And, naturally, I really became curious then. I know I had no right
to—to be so interested—because I'm sure you haven't the
slightest interest in—in—"

"Never mind." Bugs flushed. "You found this letter
tonight, huh?"

"N-no, sir . . ." The clerk's voice had sunk to a mere
whisper. "I found it . . . well, it was the night you looked
so tired. I guess you'd been up most of the day . . ."

*The day he'd gone to Westex? It must have been. Eaton had held
the letter up since then.*

". . . I opened it, Mr. McKenna. Oh, no, sir! I didn't open
the first one. I just wasn't curious enough, you know. But I
did this one, the second. And I wanted to h-help—"

"All right," Bugs said uncomfortably, "I think I understand. No sense in breaking up about it."

"I was waiting for payday, Mr. McKenna. That's the reason I held it up. I didn't want to be f-forward or embarrass
you, but I hoped you'd know that the money came from
me, and—Oh, Mr. McK-Kenna!" Eaton suddenly buried his
face in his hands. "I'm s-so ashamed. *So* ashamed!"

Bugs took the letter from his pocket, and ripped open the
envelope. There was a curt message inside:

*I want that money, Mr. McKenna, and I'm not waiting much
longer.*

There was also a fifty-dollar bill.

"Will it help any, Mr. McKenna?" Eaton looked at him
pleadingly. "I didn't know how much you might need,
but—"

"I don't need any," Bugs said flatly. "This is just a gag,
see? A bad joke that someone is pulling. I haven't quite figured out who the guy is, but I will. I can handle it, and I
want you to let me. Just keep out of it. If there are any more
of these letters, just put them in my box and forget them."

"Yes, s-sir. I'll certainly do that, Mr. McKenna. I'll—"

"I don't need any help but you do. So, goddammit, get
it!" He took fifty dollars from his wallet, added it to the
other fifty, and slapped it into the clerk's hand. "There's
bound to be a psychiatrist or a good psychologist in Westex.
Go see him and keep seeing him until you straighten
out . . . Will you do that, Les? You may have to do some

skimping on other things, but—"

"I can manage." Eaton raised his eyes. "I think my father might help. He hasn't had much use for me, but he's quite well-off—"

"Tell him what you're doing, what you're trying to do, and he'll have plenty of use." Bugs gave him a hearty slap on the back. "Meanwhile, we just forget this other. You don't know anything about it. It never happened."

"No, sir, it never happened," Eaton nodded. "But I'm awfully glad it did."

Bugs lowered the car to the first floor. He returned to the coffee shop; and Leslie Eaton, walking very straight, went back to the front offices.

. . . So now Bugs was back to Joyce Hanlon again. Joyce who had been his favorite suspect right from the start. Like Lou Ford, she couldn't openly proposition him. Like Ford, she was forcing him to show his hand before she showed hers.

She was the one person of Bugs's acquaintance who might be willing and able to do him a very substantial favor. In return, of course, he would have to do her one—the nature of which had already been indicated to him. But he must approach her in the matter. She had to be assured, before she would take him off the hook, that he would do what she wanted done.

What if he didn't approach her? If he just ignored the letters?

Well, she wasn't apt to give up that easy. She and Ford were after the old man's millions, and they'd go right on being after them. They wouldn't let a three-time loser—a pushover for a fourth fall—stand in their way. Since he wouldn't play ball, they'd put him out of the game—permanently. Make room for someone who would play on their terms.

But, hell—this was all theory. The way he *thought* things stood. And there was still that one big hole in the theory: the fact that Joyce had been in her room at the time Dudley plunged from his window.

If there was some way of explaining that . . .

Bugs finished eating. Leaving the coffee shop, he began

his long tour of the back-o'-the-house.

As usual, he wound up at about five-thirty in the morning. Yawning wearily, he sauntered into the telephone room and sank down on one of the long-legged stools.

He lighted a cigarette, stifling another yawn. The operator smiled sympathetically.

"Long night, huh, Mr. McKenna?"

"Yeah, real long. Be glad when it's time to turn in."

A light flashed on the board. She plugged it out, voiced a polite sing-song query, and made the desired connection with another plug. Then, she turned back to Bugs.

"Well, look, Mr. McKenna. If you're tired, why don't you turn in, now?"

"Yeah, why don't I?" Bugs grinned. "Suppose the old man should take a notion to ring me?"

"Suppose he did?"

"Well . . . Oh, I get you," Bugs said. "You mean he wouldn't know that I was there. You could say that you'd ring me down in the coffee shop, or something like that. Wherever I'd be likely to be at this hour of the morning."

"Uh-huh. Of course, I wouldn't do that for everyone, but someone that's all right like I know you are . . ."

Bugs stared at her vacantly. His hand moved his cigarette toward his mouth; paused in mid-air with the journey uncompleted. The operator turned away, plucked the plugs out of the board.

"I hope I didn't say anything wrong, Mr. McKenna," she murmured. "I certainly wouldn't want you to think that I go around deceiving people."

"What? Aw, no, nothing like that," Bugs protested. "No, I appreciate it. Glad to know you could help me out that way."

"Well—I don't really see that it hurts anything. After all, we're all here together, and if we can do each other a harmless little favor now and then, why—"

"Sure, that's the way I see it." Bugs veiled his eyes, fought to keep his voice casual. "But, look, let me ask you this. Suppose we just reverse the deal. I've been working too hard, say, and Hanlon orders me to stay in my room and rest up. But I don't want to do it. So I step out somewhere, and—"

"I know what you mean." The operator bobbed her head. "Well, that's an easy one. You'd just tell me where you were going to be before you left, and when he asked me to ring your room I'd ring the other place instead. I'd get you on the line, you know, and then I'd open the connection."

Bugs frowned interestedly. He remarked that a writer could make a swell plot for a story out of a situation like that. "Let's say, mmm, how could you do it? Let's—Well, how about this? You're just being nice, doing me a favor, but while I'm out of my room I commit a crime. You find out about it, and of course it's your duty to tell the cops. But if you do that, you'll put yourself on the spot. It'll cost you your job, anyway, and—"

"Oh, now, really, Mr. McKenna," the operator laughed. "I'll bet that's your secret ambition, isn't it? To be a writer?"

"Well," Bugs shrugged easily, "why not? Nothing much to it that I can see, once you've got a plot. Just putting words down on paper."

"Now, that's true, isn't it? If you've got a good idea, why, anyone could make a good story out of it. It certainly can't take any brains to do that."

"Well, getting back to this idea of mine, then. What would you do in a case like that? What would a woman do? Me, now, I don't think I'd know which way to jump. Probably figure that I'd better keep my mouth shut."

He waited. He dropped his cigarette to the floor, kept his eyes on it while he tapped it out with his foot. She was studying him, he knew. Comparing him as he was tonight with what he usually was.

For a guy who didn't ordinarily have much to say, he guessed he'd been talking a hell of a lot.

The silence grew heavier. At last he looked up, stretched lazily, and stood up.

"About your story plot, Mr. McKenna. The operator would handle hundreds of calls a night. She couldn't be expected to remember this one—I mean, the one to the place where the crime was committed."

"No? Well, probably not," Bugs agreed. "Anyway, you could hardly blame her if she didn't remember."

"And how could she know that this party she'd done the favor for had committed the crime? Just because he was there, wouldn't mean that he'd done it."

Bugs admitted that this was also right, adding, regret-fully, that he guessed his plot wasn't much good.

"Well . . . Is there anything else I can tell you?"

"No, I don't believe so," Bugs said. "I think you've told me all you can."

And with a word of good-night, he sauntered out of the room.

He hadn't learned anything definite, nothing that posi-tively placed Joyce in Dudley's room at the time of his death. Under the circumstances, however, the fact that she could have been there was good evidence that she had been. Dudley was pretty lowdown. He could easily have been pulling a squeeze-play on her of some kind, and got squeezed himself.

Yeah, it figured, all right. The facts added up despite their one nominal contradiction. Joyce couldn't move directly against her husband because of his money—the danger-ously strong motive it represented. But there'd be no such obstacle in the way of her doing a job on Dudley.

The end of the shift came, and Bugs went to bed. As usual, he spent the evening with Amy, another evening that was at once wonderful yet insidiously aggravating.

He left early, and a little huffily. Returning to his room, he called Joyce Hanlon.

She was pretty cool when she first came to his room. She'd tried to be nice to him, she pointed out. She'd got him his job, and then she'd done her best to see that he made out okay. And in return he'd given her a good hard snubbing. Well, she didn't take that kind of stuff. She didn't have to take it from anyone, and she particularly didn't have to take it from a guy like him. *Particularly,* understand? And he could take that any way he wanted to.

Bugs let her get the mad out of her system. Now; finally, she lay stretched out on the bed, knees drawn up, one long silken leg stretched over the other. She was puffing a cigarette, lazily blowing smoke toward the ceiling. Asking a question with her silence, and preparing herself for the answer.

She was like a cat, Bugs thought. Perfectly relaxed, yet ready to spring instantly in any direction.

He cleared his throat, fidgeted uncertainly in his chair. He said, "Joyce . . . I want to ask you something."

"Mmm-hmm?"

"You don't really need five thousand dollars do you?"

"Five thou—Well," she laughed with deliberate lightness. "Every little five thousand helps, you know. Five thousand here and five thousand there, and—"

"You know what I mean. You don't want five thousand from me."

"We-ell . . . I'd be rather foolish if I did, wouldn't I? A case of wanting in one hand and spitting in the other."

"Now, dammit, Joyce listen—!"

"I'm trying to, Bugs. Very hard. I'm sure if you say anything I'll hear it."

Bugs hesitated, leaned forward. "I've been getting letters. They demand five thousand dollars as a price for keeping quiet about a certain matter. You've been writing them."

"Have I? Now, how could you possibly think a thing like that?"

"Because this matter concerns Dudley—his death. Because I know you were with him at the time."

"Oh," she said. "So that's where I was."

She raised up on one elbow, dropped her cigarette into an ashtray. She lay back down again, drowsily shielding her eyes with the back of her hand.

"There's only one way you could be so sure of that, Bugs. You were with him, too."

"Well—let's say I'm not sure of it. Only as sure as you're sure about me. It's a push, in other words. You can't put me any further into the soup than I can put you into it."

"Mmm, I don't believe you really think that way, do you, honey? If you did, you wouldn't be worried about those letters I'm supposedly writing you."

"Maybe I'm just smarter than you are," Bugs said. "maybe you ought to be worried a lot more."

"Now that," Joyce murmured, "is a straight line if I ever

heard one. Coming from a guy with a record like yours—"

"What about your record? And don't tell me you haven't got one."

"But I haven't, darling. Honestly."

"Nuts. You're no kid, and Dudley couldn't be the first guy you hit with that stuff. It's a modus operandi, the trade-mark of a certain type of worker. Some gals go in for boosting, or paper-pushing or lifting leathers. Others work the chloral hydrate."

That did it, jarred her out of the indifferent act. Her body stiffened, and under the shielding fingers, her eyes widened with sudden fear. She lay almost absolutely motionless for a moment. Then she slowly sat up, swung her feet to the floor.

Bugs grinned at her. She looked at him blankly; and then her lips twisted into a different kind of grin.

"Yes," she said, "some gals work the chloral hydrate. Hard-boiled gals. Gals who'll take the long chance . . . So that alleged record of mine isn't much protection for you, is it, Bugs? No more than I care to let it be. And if I don't care to let it be at all . . ."

"Then you'd be stupid?"

"Perhaps. Under different circumstances. But you've got a pretty good idea that those circumstances don't exist in this case, that there isn't going to be any matching up of records. The lightning is going to strike in just one spot, and you'll be on it. That's your idea—your pretty good idea—and it's a pretty good idea to hang onto."

"You're talking about Ford, now. He'll protect you."

"That sounds reasonable, doesn't it? But you're saying it, Bugs. I haven't said a word."

"But dammit," Bugs snapped. "You're not telling me anything. I can't be sure where Ford stands or—or—"

"You should be able to. All you have to do is see how he runs this town, remember the way he picked you up out of nowhere and brought you to me . . . I'd say he was a very pleasant easy-going guy when it suits him. He couldn't ignore something if it was shoved right in his face, but—"

"You're still not telling me anything! Now, let's have it, Joyce. What do you want—what am I supposed to do—and how can I be sure I'll get away with it?"

She laughed softly, with false sweetness. Crinkled her eyes at him coquettishly. "Why, Bugs. I believe that's the nicest compliment I've ever had. Of course, I do think I hold my age very well, but—"

"Compliment! What—"

"Mmm-hmm. Saying I was only a day old. Or isn't that what you meant—that I was born yesterday?"

She laughed again, but in a different way. Amused. Jeering. Then she stood up, swinging the sable stole back around her shoulders.

"You've taken your time about seeing me, Bugs, and now you don't have anything to say. But—never mind. I'm sure you won't wait so long next time, will you? I'll hear from you very, very soon, because otherwise my feelings might be hurt. And if that happened . . ."

Bugs let out a moaning snarl of frustration. He again asked what the hell she wanted him to say. Or rather he started to. She cut him off with a thoughtful gesture.

"I've been thinking, Bugs . . . Why bother to say anything? It isn't at all necessary, is it?"

Bugs looked into her mocking face. He shrugged wearily and was silent.

"At least, a word or two should be enough. Don't you think? . . . Okay? All right?"

She left then, leaving the words hanging in the air.

Bugs bathed his face in ice water and went dully to work. He'd botched things, he guessed. He'd as good as admitted that he'd been in Dudley's room, while she, on the other hand had admitted nothing. And there was no satisfaction at all in the possibility that she might be bluffing, taking advantage of the blackmail act which another person was pulling.

Because someone *was* pulling it. And whether it was Joyce who wanted her husband murdered, or whether it was another woman who merely *(merely!)* wanted five grand, he was still behind the eight ball. Either way, a demand was being made on him that could only be met in one way.

But he knew it had to be Joyce. He was sure of it, and he became surer. For there were no more of the blackmail letters. And if she hadn't been sending them . . . well, they would have continued, wouldn't they?

Bugs could see it in no other way. Joyce had made her point. Having made it, the letters became unnecessary. Now, she was waiting, checking the next move to him.

As the days dragged by—she began to prod him toward that move. No, she still didn't come out in the open. She said or did nothing even remotely incriminating. It was just a matter of an occasional telephone call, or a brief visit to his room. No more than the open and patently innocent friendliness she had showed for him from the beginning. How was he feeling—okay? How was he getting along—all right? Well, that was fine. And so on, and so on.

Bugs grew more and more tense. He was a bundle of worries and nerves, hardly able to keep his mind on his job, almost wholly unable to rest or relax. He couldn't take any more, he thought. He'd have to give in, give up, or—

And he didn't know how. He was incapable of it. As his tension and worry and fear increased, so did his stubbornness.

No crooked cop was pushing him around. No two-bit floozy was giving him orders. No one was making him do a goddamned thing that he didn't want to do.

That's the way it was. That's the way it had been all his life. And if anyone didn't like it, they knew what they could do about it. They might kill him, but they wouldn't change him. They might give him a beating, but they'd damned sure know they'd been in a fight.

So there was a stalemate, one which no amount of subtly insistent threats from Joyce could jar him out of. One which would remain—in his own mind, at least—until he himself decided to change it. His instinct for survival tangled with unrelenting stubbornness; and subconsciously relishing the situation, revelling in a feeling of nobility and martyrdom, he would neither retreat nor go forward.

In the end, he resolved the stalemate himself. For the same reason—and as harrowingly as—he had done so with countless others. Because he was tired of it. Because he had gotten all the self-torturing pleasure from it that could possibly be extracted. Being what he was, however, he could not admit this.

It was Amy's doing, not his. It was Amy who, while he

was tottering right on the brink, gave him a push.

If Amy had been fair . . .

If she'd been understanding . . .

If she'd been forgiving . . .

If she'd been a saint instead of another human like himself . . .

If she'd been willing to take everything he dished out, meanwhile whimpering with adoration and self-abnegation . . .

Well, that was really all he expected of her. Although he wouldn't have put it quite that way.

Afterwards, when he had acquired a reasonably normal perspective, he couldn't understand how he could have acted as he had, how any grown man could have behaved in such a determinedly boorish and uningratiating manner. He had been given no excuse to behave that way, nothing that could be sanely regarded as an excuse. On the contrary, Amy showed much less spirit and independence than she usually did. She smiled at provocative statements. She laughed off near-insults. She petted him, literally and figuratively, when she must have felt like clouting him.

And somehow it only made Bugs worse. The greater her efforts to please him, the greater were his to be displeased—and displeasing. With part of his mind he was aware of this; he knew he was utterly wrong, and getting wronger by the minute. But he just couldn't help it. He was like a man in a dream, delighting in deeds which at the same time sickened and shocked him.

Amy had cooked liver for their dinner. It was not a dish that Bugs had any very strong feelings about either way. But tonight he decided to dislike it. So after a few obviously reluctant bites, he pushed his plate aside.

Yeah, he mumbled unconvincingly, it was okay. All right. Just wasn't very hungry, he guessed.

"Oh, I'm sorry. Aren't you feeling well, Mac?"

"Yeah, sure, I'm feeling well. Why not? I just said I

wasn't hungry."

"I guess I should have got something else," she said apologetically. "I meant to, but they were having a special on
liver today, and, oh, you know how it is with a woman! Just
can't pass up a bargain. Of course, if I'd known that you
didn't like—"

"Amy, for—! Never mind, have your own way about it."

"I'm sorry, honey," she smiled quickly. "I won't say
another word. If you're not hungry, you're not, and why
should you eat when you're not?"

Bugs managed to say that he was sorry, too. But he didn't
sound like he meant it—and he didn't. Except with that
very small part of his mind. She was picking on him, he
told himself. She, of all people, was finding fault with *him!*

He drank coffee and smoked a cigarette while she hurried
through her meal. He studied her out of brooding, sultry
eyes.

She looked childishly young tonight, like a gay, friendly
child in a woman's body. Her clear peaches-and-cream skin
was free of make-up. Her candy-colored hair was pulled
back in a horse's-tail. Beneath their silky brown lashes, her
gray eyes were straight forward and sparkling.

She was wearing a housedress. Neat, stiffly starched and
immaculately clean, yet faded and shrunken. It barely came
to her knees, fitted snugly over the curves of her body. Her
full breasts strained against the material, were pushed
upward by its tightness. And Bugs could see deep into the
hollow between them.

He stared, almost openly, feeling a surge in his unreason-
ing resentment. He wanted her, wanted to look upon her
again as he had looked upon her that first time, and the
desire made him furious. What was she trying to pull, anyway? What was the idea in appearing so damned girlish
and innocent when they both knew that she wasn't?

He continued to stare. Gradually, a slow flush spread
over her face, and her hand moved timidly to the front of
her dress, tried to narrow the gap of its neckline.

"I'll bet I look a sight," she murmured self-consciously. "I
was racing around all day cleaning house, and I didn't have
time to fix myself up. I—I usually plan things better. But I
guess I've gotten kind of off-schedule since I quit working,

and—Mac," she said, "Mac . . . what's the matter, darling?"

Darling. Dear. Honey. That's what she was calling him these days. The same names she had used to call Ford—if she wasn't still doing it.

"Matter?" he said. "What do you mean?"

"Well—you know. Why are you looking at me like that?"

"Like what?" Bugs shrugged. "Just thinking, I guess. Wondering how you were getting along with Ford these days."

"But"—she set down her coffee cup nervously. "I don't see Lou any more, honey. I told you that."

"Yeah, I guess you did tell me that, didn't you?" he said deliberately. "Haven't figured out where he gets his money yet, have you?"

"Mac . . ." She put a hand over his. "Let's not talk about that again tonight, please? You'll just get upset, and it won't change anything—"

"I don't know how you can do it!" he raged suddenly. "He's running a wide-open town, isn't he? He's rolling in dough, isn't he? You know he is, and you know he can't be drawing much more than three thousand dollars salary a year. And yet you sit there and tell me he isn't a crook!"

"Please, dear. Can't we just—"

"Why don't you admit it?" He jerked his hand from beneath hers. "Why do you go on defending him? Why, when you've got all the facts right in front of you, do you—"

"Mac, I've tried to explain. The town's always been more or less open, as you put it. The people want it that way. They'd never vote taxes to stop something that they see no real harm in. And with so many thousands of newcomers . . . well, you can understand how it is, honey. How can one man with a few deputies do anything but what he is doing? Just keeping things out in the open where they can be watched, and keeping them under control."

"Oh, sure, sure. I've heard that yarn before. Every crooked cop in the country has the same alibi."

"I don't say it's right, Mac. I don't believe Lou thinks it is. But he's realistic, and—"

"And he's got a nice thing going for himself."

She looked at him steadily, almost without expression, for a moment. Slowly, she pushed her plate back, spoke in a quiet, even voice.

"I don't know where Lou's money comes from, Mac. I never asked. He never explained—presumably for good reasons of his own. No, wait"—she held up a hand. "Let me finish. When I say good reasons I mean it literally. Because whatever else Lou is, he is honest. I know he is. So does everyone else who's known him for any length of time."

"But that doesn't make sense!" Bugs insisted surlily. "If he—"

"All right, it doesn't make sense, then. But it's still the truth."

Bugs scowled and jabbed out his cigarette. Amy studied him, her gray eyes defiant, debating something within herself. There was a fiddle-string tautness about the silence. A feeling of tension mounting to the breaking point. Then, she smiled and it was as though the sun had come out from behind a cloud. And, grudgingly, Bugs found himself smiling back.

Grudgingly, yet with a vast sense of relief . . .

Amy came around the table and kissed him on the forehead. She tousled his hair, fondly, her lips curved with a kind of dreamy softness. It was very peaceful. Never in his life had he known such peace. Then, abruptly, he pulled her down into his lap.

"Amy . . ." he said. "Amy, I—"

"Tell me about it, darling. Tell me . . ." Her warm mouth brushed lovingly against his cheek. "It'll be all right, whatever it is. If it isn't, we'll make it all right."

"Nothing," Bugs said. "I mean—"

And there was no longer anything. Or, rather, that is all there was. Anything, something. Not someone, but something. Buttocks, and breasts, and thighs and—

He was crushing her mouth with his. Pawing and clutching and grasping at her. One hand was thrust high beneath the prim little dress, roamed there crudely and cruelly. And one of her breasts filled his other hand. And—and she was silent and unprotesting. She said nothing, made no movement of her own. She merely looked at him.

He released her suddenly and shoved her to her feet. He jumped up and started for the door, paused without turning around.

"Well," he said gruffly. "Why don't you say it? Might as well say it as think it."

"I thought there might be something you wanted to say, Mac . . ." She waited a moment. "But, anyway, I'm not sure what I think. So, perhaps . . ."

"Yeah?"

"Perhaps there's nothing to be said. Why don't you go on in the living-room, and I'll be with you as soon as I stack the dishes."

He went in and sat down. She joined him after a few minutes, and again apparently she had decided to forget and forgive. It was all right, she told him with her eyes, her smile, her warmth. He hadn't meant what he'd seemed to, and she knew that he hadn't.

She sat down at his side on the lounge. She talked, talking for both of them, trying to bring him out of himself. Then she played a few pieces on the piano, singing in her soft sweet voice. And nothing seemed to help. The bitter blackness crept slowly upward and around him.

What's wrong with me? he thought a little wildly, with that small rational segment of his mind. *She's all I've got, the only thing left to cling to, all that really matters. Everything else is headed for hell on a handcar, and now I'm trying to pile her on too. And—*

"Mac . . ." She was seated at his side again. "I don't like to keep asking you, but—"

He glared at her silently, daring her to ask again if he was in any kind of trouble. She left the sentence unfinished, moved smoothly to another topic.

He'd never been through the house, had he? Well, there was nothing much to see, of course, but if he'd like to look around . . .

They began with the basement, with its faint sweet-sour smell of straw and apples and earth. From there they went up the back stairs to the attic—huge, ghostly and shadowed with the discards of by-gone days—and then down to the second floor.

Amy led the way from room to room, determinedly

friendly, fighting with everything she had against his growing ugliness.

Once she asked him how he liked the place, how he would like to live in a big old-fashioned house like this one. Another time she said she supposed she'd have to sell it, since there was no work for her here in Ragtown, and she hardly knew where else to go, or what she would do if she did go somewhere else. She'd always lived here, and her folks had always lived here, and—

"This was their room." She opened the door of the largest room, one with two four-poster double beds. "Poor darlings they had an awfully hard time of it. Dad fell off a horse and broke his back, and he was bedfast until he died. And Mother, she was never quite the same after he passed on. She lost interest in everything, and—"

...And, God, he thought, *that must have been hard on you, honey. Harder than anything I went through with my folks. They meant well, even if they did do a lot toward mixing me up. And they didn't ask anything of me, and I didn't have much to give them—or anyone—if I'd been asked. But you, a girl like you, gay and full of life and pretty as a picture—you, tied down out here in the prairie nowhere, tied to two dying people, watching the years slip away from you . . .*

That was the way his thoughts ran. But he said . . .

He wasn't quite sure what he said—the wording of it. But the sense of it was clear enough.

She looked up at him slowly, white-faced, eyes sick with shock. Then, without a word she led the way out of the room and into her own.

She gestured toward a spindle-legged love-seat, covered with faded pink satin. He sat down on it, started to make room for her, and she sat down on a straight-backed chair.

"Now, about the questions you asked, Mac," she said quietly. "The answer to the—"

"Never mind," Bugs grunted. "I wasn't thinking how—"

"—the answer to the first one is, yes. I hadn't thought much about it, but I suppose that his father and my parents being invalided for so long, did give Lou and me a strong common bond. As to the second question, the answer is no. Our parents' illness did not make things convenient for us. We didn't take advantage of it for the purpose you implied. In fact—"

"Skip it," Bugs growled uncomfortably. "I—I didn't mean that the way it sounded."

"Of course, you mean it. You've been working up to it ever since we became acquainted. I can't blame you, I suppose, although I am disappointed and hurt. I hoped you'd accept me without question, as I've been willing to accept you. Since you can't do that, however, I'm going to tell you something . . ."

. . .She had thought she was in love with Lou Ford, made herself believe that she was. And she had clung to him, chased him, fought to hold onto him, despite his determination not to be held and the obvious fact that he was wholly unsuited to married life. For, you see, she had felt that she must marry him. She had never gone with any other men. She had been unable to marry at an age when most girls did; and now he was the one remaining eligible, the one man of her own kind. And without him—as she saw it—there would be nothing. No real reason for existence. None of the things that make life worth living. Only a yawning, lonely emptiness, stretching endlessly through the endless years ahead.

It had seemed an unbearable prospect. She had persuaded herself that it must be avoided, at whatever cost. And Lou Ford had led her to believe that it might be . . . in a certain way. So she had been ready to submit to him, and when she was, he had laughed at her. Jeered and teased her. Some other time, he had grinned. After all, that stuff was pretty cheap, could be, anyways. Why toss hers away when she might need it later?

Her immediate reaction was one of outrage, murderous anger. It had taken her a few days to see the way of what he had done; that in his shaming of her, his calculated cruelty, he had reinstated her sense of values so securely that they could never be shaken loose again. He had demonstrated that no matter how nominally desirable a thing may be, its price *can* be too high—and it is too high if the payment bankrupts the purchaser—and he had driven that message home, with painful emphasis, on several later occasions. She had resented the lesson; doubtless, she was still a little resentful. But she knew he was right, and after she met

Bugs . . .

"I did a pretty cheap thing, Mac; one that I'll always be ashamed of. And it's not my fault that I didn't do something a lot cheaper. But it is all I did. There was nothing more than . . . well just what you saw."

"You mean," Bugs frowned. "You mean you were nak—you had your clothes off, and you didn't—uh—"

"That's what I mean. Don't you believe me?"

"Well," he shrugged. "Well, sure, if you say so." He ran a hand across his mouth, but not quite quickly enough. Not quickly enough to conceal the smirk of incredulity. "Well, sure," he repeated. "Of course, you have to admit it sounds kind of, uh—"

"Funny? Is that what you were going to say, Mac? Well, perhaps you're right. It is funny. And now that I think of it, there's something still funnier."

She got up and moved toward the door. He arose, too, thinking that she was leaving. But instead she closed the door, and turned off the light.

And in the faint moonlight which drifted through the window, he saw her body arched delicately as she drew her dress off over her head. She felt her way across the room, shedding her other garments, leaving them where they fell.

The bed creaked, and she said, "All right, Mac."

His mouth felt very dry. He licked his lips, and stammered, "Aw, no, Amy. It doesn't make any difference, even if—"

"Even. If," she said. "Come on."

Well. If that was the way she wanted it, you couldn't blame him. After all he was a man, and a man couldn't help being like he was made. And a man expected, and had a right to expect, a woman to be better than he was.

So . . .

So.

Bugs still knew very little about women. But by now he knew at least enough to realize that Amy had spoken the truth. And along with the inevitable ecstasy of his union with her, there was also abysmal shame and soul-sickening terror—terror of the loss he had suffered. For, naturally, he had lost her. He knew it even before he arose from the bed, from the hateful triumph over her body.

"Amy, I want to tell you something. I—"

"I don't want to hear it," she said. "Just get out."

"But—but I didn't mean it. I am in trouble; it's got me half out of my mind. I didn't want to tell you about it because—"

"Because you didn't trust me. Because there's nothing in you to trust or love or understand with. Just a lot of hatred and grudges and suspicion. N-now" —shakily she started to rise, her voice rising. "Now, you get out! Get out and don't ever come back! Don't ever come near me or try to—"

"Amy. If you'll only—"

"Do you hear me? *GET OUT!*"

She advanced on him, eyes wild, small fists drawn back. He grabbed up his clothes, and fled into the hallway.

He dressed out in the hall, hopping clumsily from one foot to the other, getting his shirt buttoned the wrong way, snapping a shoestring—making a botch of things generally in his haste to escape. In his mind's eye he stood off from himself, examined the hulking, red-faced, panting and fumbling figure in the hallway. And it was as though he was staring into a fun-house mirror. He felt preposterously small and futile. He was livid with shame and embarrassment.

He hated himself, and he hated her for making him hate himself.

He dressed and was out of the house in a few minutes—minutes that seemed like hours. He stopped at the first bar he came to, tossed down five drinks in a row. And when he left he took a pint bottle with him. He went to the hotel, to his room, and began drinking.

The booze didn't get him drunk; there wasn't enough whiskey in Ragtown to get him drunk that night. It merely intensified his fury, increased and compressed it until it was like a great rat, trapped in a tiny corner, raging insanely for the release of action.

But not tonight, he thought. Not—not any more tonight. But tomorrow night . . .

He would do it tomorrow night. Do something. Move decisively and irrevocably one way or another.

There was a soft rapping on his door, a familiar shave-and-a-haircut-six-bits knock. Grinning grimly, he got up and opened it, closed and locked it again as Joyce brushed past him. He moved back into the room with her, looked her up and down slowly as she turned and faced him.

"Well, Bugs?"

"Yeah?" He moved closer to her, backing her against the bed. "Yeah, Joyce?"

"Well"—she smiled nervously—"uh, nothing. I just stopped by to—to—"

"To see how I was getting along," he nodded. "To see how I was feeling. Well, I'm plumb glad you asked, as your buddy Lou Ford would say. I'm plain tickled that you came by, and that's a fact. Because—"

"Bugs—*don't* you've been drinking, and—"

"—because I feel pretty low-down. About as low-down as a man can get. And that don't quite bring me down to your level, of course, but it's close enough. I can't crawl under the plank with you, but—"

"You rotten crazy bastard!" Her palm cracked against his face. "I'll—I'm getting out of here!"

"Without your clothes, you mean? You go right ahead, but the clothes won't be going. Not if you leave before I say you can. Well"—he got a grip on the front of her dress. "What's it going to be?"

She bit her lip, forced a tremulous smile. Her hand moved coyly to his chest, twisted one of the misbuttoned buttons.

"Aw, Bugs. This isn't any way for my Bugsy boy to act. What's got into you, anyway, honey?"

"That isn't the question. Not what's got into me, but what's about to—"

She snickered unwillingly. A strange excitement began to dance in her eyes. Still, she liked to call the shots; she'd gotten used to doing it. And she'd almost forgotten the days when things were different—painfully so—and the exquisite pleasure to be derived from that painful difference.

It was dim in her mind. Growing clearer, but not quite

recognized as yet.

"Let's not, Bugs, hmm? No, really, I mean it. I absolutely refuse, and you can't make me! You—"

"Can't I?" he said. His fingers dug into her flesh. "Can't I, Joyce? Can't—"

"B-Bugs . . ." A great shiver ran through her body, "Bugs! Y-you're—you're . . . Ahhhhhhh . . ."

. . . She lay sprawled on the bed, breathing in deep luxurious breaths. Exhausted, depleted, replenished. Bugs sat on the bed's edge, smoking moodily in the darkness. Thinking that no matter how low a man went, there was always another low awaiting him. Even after this there was doubtless another one. And doubtless he would descend to it, and for as little reason as he had descended to this one, and the one immediately preceding it.

"Bugs, honey . . ." She found his hand, and he jerked it rudely away. "Maybe afterwards—after things are settled— we could clear out of this place. Go away somewhere together."

"The nearest whorehouse, that's as far as I'll go with you. Park you there and put you to work."

"Aw, now, Bugs. Not that I wouldn't if it was necessary. I'd do anything for you, honey. But—"

"What makes you so sure it won't be? Where else do you think you're going to get any dough?"

"Huh!" She sat up abruptly. "What the hell do you mean where . . . Oh"—She broke off, seeing the sardonic jeer on his face, went back to her former meekness. "It isn't just me, Bugs. If it was just up to me, I'd never think of trying to—uh—persuade you to do anything that you didn't want to. But—"

"Sure. Just like you haven't been trying to."

"But I can't help it, honey. You know that. There's another person involved. What I want or don't want, doesn't really make much difference."

Bugs tossed his cigarette into a tray. He squared around on the bed a little, sat looking down into her face.

"All right," he said. "We'll say it's that way. But now you're going to tell me something. No more of this damned hinting and beating around the bush, get me? No more of this am-I-all-right and how-am-I-feeling stuff. You're going to come right out and tell me what you do want. I want to hear you say it."

"B-but—but you already know, honey. Why should I—"

"I said, I wanted to hear you say it! Spit it out. Do it and do it fast, or I'm through, so—*Shut up! Don't threaten me or I'll break your goddamned neck!*— so make up your mind. Say it or drop it."

"But—"

Her head moved irritably against the pillows. She took a deep breath and held it; then, slowly let it out again in a quiet sigh of surrender.

"All right, Bugs," she said. "All right, darling. You don't trust me, but I'll still—"

"Out with it!"

"I want you to kill him. I want you to kill my husband!"

. . . There was a kind of peace on this new level at which he found himself. Uneasy but still soothing, and peculiarly satisfying. Marvelously trouble-free compared with the black turmoil he had come through.

He had known such peace before. Experiencing it now he wondered why it must be so insistently impinged upon by the leering image of Chief Deputy Lou Ford. Because, of course, Ford was all wrong about him. The deputy had apparently dug deeply into his background, excavated the facts behind the bleak syllabus of the police record. And he'd twisted the annals of Bugs's life into that seemingly factual but cruelly and viciously distorted, case-history which he had recited to Bugs several days ago.

He *made* trouble for himself, Ford had said. He deliberately plunged himself into one scrape after another. In so doing, he bulwarked his self-pitying conviction that the whole world was against him—and it was a hell of a lot more fun, as well as a hell of a lot easier, than doing something constructive.

There was that dame he had married, for example. Yeah, sure, he was a greenhorn when it came to women, but that was no excuse. A ten-year-old boy—anyone that had sense enough to come in out of the rain—would have known that she had to be a tramp. And he, Bugs, had damned well known it, even if he wouldn't admit it. He'd simply stuck his neck out because he liked being hit over the head.

Another example: that screwball detective Bugs had shot. Now, here was a guy who was obviously dangerous, and who obviously had a pick on him. Yet Bugs hadn't done a damned thing to forestall the disaster which he must have foreseen. He'd just hung around waiting for the lightning to strike.

Pride? Guts? Balls! He wouldn't kick a skunk, would he? Or lie down next to a rattlesnake? Making a damned fool of yourself didn't take pride or guts, did it? Well, then.

Ford had had a lot more to say, but it was all in the same vein. He liked being in jams. He'd rather have things go bad than good.

Which, of course, was screwy on the face of it, Bugs thought angrily. Anyone could see that it was. It had just been some more of Ford's whipcracking, pouring in on him because he knew he had to take it. The guy couldn't open his mouth without needling someone. And when that someone was really under his thumb . . .

Bugs finished his shift. He went to bed, slightly hungover from the booze he had drunk, grasping at that strange, uneasy peace which kept slipping away from him. He started to doze, and a disturbing thought pushed into his mind. Clung there stubbornly, forcing him back into wakefulness:

Everything was going fine. No trouble. No way for anyone to make trouble. And then I went to Dudley's room. Ollie had no right to ask me to; he couldn't have honestly expected me to. But I went, anyway. Knowing that it wouldn't do any good to talk to Dudley. Knowing that I didn't dare to do anything more than talk. Boiling it down, I didn't have to go, and I didn't have any reason for going. And yet—

Bugs squirmed irritably and flopped over on his back. He lay scowling, eyes squinted, staring up at the ceiling.

Suppose there had been no woman in Dudley's bathroom. Suppose Dudley hadn't gone out the window. Wasn't it still pretty likely that he'd have gotten into trouble? In fact, wasn't it virtually inevitable that he would have?

And hadn't he known that he would at the time he went to the room?

Well?

Well . . . Of course not! It was easy to second guess on a deal, to see where you'd goofed after you'd done it. If he'd known it was going to land him in a scrape, why—

He rolled over on his side again. He burrowed his head into the pillow, closed his eyes firmly, and kept them closed. At last, he slept, And when he awakened, it was night. *The* night.

Mike Hanlon was in the bathroom when Bugs arrived at his suite. Braced against the sink, he finished washing his hands, then sank back down into his wheelchair and rolled himself out into the living-room.

"Well, Bugs"—his shrewd old eyes swept over Bugs's face. "We get our tour at last, huh? I was beginning to think you'd forgot all about me."

"No. No, I hadn't forgotten." Bugs looked away from him. "I—well, I just kept putting it off, and—"

"Sure, I understand. Well, I'll be with you in a minute or two. Help yourself to a drink while you're waiting."

Bugs decided he could use a drink. He poured a stiff shot from a nearby carafe, and took it into the bathroom. He added ice water to it, gulped it with a shudder. As he bent over to draw another glass, his head bumped lightly against the medicine cabinet and its mirrored door swung open.

Sipping the water, he stared absently at the crowded shelves of nostrums. One bottle was sitting right on the edge of its shelf, in danger of falling off. He pushed it back inside, then, frowning unconsciously, continued to stare at it for a moment longer.

It was almost empty. The liquid in the bottom was a clear white, and had an oily look about it. Bugs couldn't say why it interested him, subtly disturbed him. Any number of medicines were a clear white, and oily looking. But still . . .

He was reaching for it, starting to turn it around to examine the label. But Hanlon called to him at that moment, so he closed the door and went back into the living-room.

He wheeled the invalid out into the hall. Unlocking the door of the elevator he had appropriated, he switched on the light and wheeled him inside.

"I see you haven't forgotten my preference for lighted elevators," Hanlon grinned. "Not that I'd ever be worried, of course, about you being careless."

"Yeah." Bugs closed the door, turning his back to him. "Where'd you like to start, Mr. Hanlon?"

"We-el . . . how about the roof?"

Bugs nodded silently. He was calm enough, not afraid to speak. But the words somehow would not form themselves; and something whispered that it was best to leave them unformed. As much as possible, Hanlon should do the talking.

They reached the roof. Bugs wheeled him out of the car and across the tiled floor to the guard-wall, and they looked out over the oil fields.

Bugs didn't think. There was plenty of time. Nothing needed to be done or decided now. In this moment all there was was this: he and the old man, and the night, and the blazing, thundering jungle of steel.

Flame licked the sky from a thousand flambeaux. The huge torches—set up to consume excess gas—were everywhere, barely burning at one moment, then suddenly ripping the darkness with a fifty-foot spear of flame.

". . . still smell like rotten eggs to you, Bugs?"

"Huh? No, I guess it doesn't. Got to where I kind of like it."

"Thought you would," Hanlon murmured. "I mean, how can you dislike a thing like that? Anything that comes from the oil. Because . . . well, maybe people got hurt the way I went after it. But damned little, relatively. And most of 'em profited in the long run. Y'know—" he laughed a little sadly. It'll sound funny to you, but that was originally what attracted me to the business. You could help yourself in it— get rich maybe—without hurting other people. You didn't have to squeeze 'em. You didn't have to push them down to push yourself up. All you had to do was find the oil, and everyone was better off, and no one was hurt . . . unless it was you."

"Yeah? Yes, sir?" Bugs said.

"Yes. Because there's one thing a man needs damned bad if he hits it rich, and it's the one thing he can't buy. He can't buy someone he can trust. If he could . . . do you think he could, Bugs? Do you think if I bought a man—offered any price he named within reason—that he'd stay bought?"

He waited, looking up into Bugs's face. Bugs shrugged silently, indifferently. But his heart quickened its beat.

"Well," Hanlon sighed. "Well, that's that, I guess."

They remained at the guard-wall for a few minutes longer. Then Hanlon peered around in the darkness, gestured toward a shadowy mass a dozen or so feet away. "That's where the remodeling is going on, isn't it? The terrace extension? Well, let's go over and have a look at it."

Bugs pulled the chair back from the wall and wheeled him down the tiles. They reached the array of building materials and tools, and Bugs paused to let him look around. He waited a minute or two, then started to resume pushing. The old man stopped him quickly.

"Nothing to see over there, I guess. Just more brick and lumber."

"Whatever you say," Bugs said.

"Let's see, now. I wonder if you could squeeze me through this stuff, and out to the terrace. Ought to be a good view from there."

"Well, yeah, I guess there is. But . . ."

He stared down at Hanlon, eyes blank and dull. He seemed to stand there for hours, hesitating, yet it was not even a split second. For there was no decision to reach, nothing to make up his mind about. That had all been done right in the beginning.

"Just a minute," he said. "I'll see how it looks."

He moved a wheelbarrow out of the way and went down a narrow aisle between some cement sacks and a long mixing-trough. At the terrace doors, he pushed two stacked saw-horses aside and pulled them open. He took a cautious step or two forward, came to an abrupt stop.

Ahead of him, there was a breach in the guard-rail: an open door into emptiness. On the left, where the terrace was being extended, the rail had been completely removed.

A man would have to be damned careful out here. And even then, in the deceptive darkness, it would be easy to . . .

Bugs hesitated, deliberating. Then, he went back through the doors and returned to Hanlon.

"Guess we better not," he said. "Too dangerous."

"*Dangerous!* But—"

"Yeah. You might wind up down in the street. I'll just block those doors again, and—"

"Bugs!" Hanlon cut him off sharply. "Bugs, I want to go out there, and I know that you—I mean, there isn't a thing for you to worry about. I'll take the responsibility. Everyone knows that I like to have my own way, and—and—"

He looked up at Bugs with a kind of wheedling eagerness. He waited. The eagerness fading, giving way to something else; and then he laughed nervously, and shifted his gaze. "This damned robe"— he plucked it from his lap. "Don't need it any more than—ha, ha—that gun I had with me last time. Should've left it back in my suite with the gun. I—Okay, Bugs. Well?"

"Well?" Bugs said. "Look, Mr. Hanlon, I guess we'd better be shoving off. I've got work to do, and—"

"Wait!" The old man gripped the wheels of his chair, holding them motionless. "What's the matter? I told you it'd be all right, didn't I? I showed you. You won't be taking any risk at all, and . . ."

His voice trailed off into silence, and one hand went up to his face, rubbed it shakily; and he heaved a tired and wondering sigh.

"Bugs," he quavered. "I-I don't know how to say it. I . . . I was right, wasn't I, Bugs? Right and all wrong. You can't buy a man, and you don't have to. All you have to do is—" His voice broke. He sighed again and went on. "You'll stay here in Ragtown, won't you, Bugs? Stay with the hotel? I'm not trying to buy you, but you're capable of something a lot better than a house-dick's job. And—"

Bugs shook his head in honest bewilderment. For consciously he could not understand. Briefly, his path had run parallel to an abyss of evil; but now it was aeons behind him. It was a bad all-but-forgotten dream, rather than a one-time reality.

"I'm sorry Bugs," Hanlon said apologetically. "I should have known you wouldn't do it. You couldn't. You couldn't commit a cold-blooded murder."

"Told you so myself"—Lou Ford's voice drifted out of the darkness. "Too bad I can't say the same for you, Mis-ter Hanlon."

Trailed by another deputy, he emerged from behind a pile of brick. He sauntered up to Bugs and Hanlon, flicking the head from a match, touching the flame to the tip of his cigar.

"Yes, sir," he grinned easily at Bugs. "I told him you wouldn't. Catch *you* doing anything that anyone wanted you to."

Bugs stared at him dumbly, hardly hearing what he said, still trying to digest what Hanlon had said. Ford's grin changed imperceptibly, and for a moment the bite went out of his voice.

"You wouldn't do it, period," he said. "Just ain't built that way. Now, Mis-ter Hanlon here, he could do it—probably make a pretty slick job of it too. F'r example, he could make out like he was scared to death hisself, and while he had the law lookin' the other way—"

"That's enough!" Hanlon snapped. "I made a mistake, and I'm damned glad it was one. However, if you feel that you've been imposed upon, that I've taken your time up needlessly, why, just say so and I'll give you a tip."

"A big one?" Ford asked in an awed tone. "Maybe a big shiny two-bit piece? Aw, gee, Mis-ter Hanlon . . . What do you think, Al? A whole two-bitses to divvy up between us!"

"Makes my mouth plumb water," the other deputy drawled. "Prob'ly go hog wild and spend it all in one place."

Ford chuckled. Hanlon let out an angry snarl. "I said to cut it out! Go pull your clown act somewhere else! I don't have to take it, and I'm not going to!"

"Well, okay," Ford said sadly. "I guess if we don't get our two-bits and you ain't even going to offer us a drink . . . Did your wife have a drink with you tonight, Mis-ter Hanlon?"

"Did she have a drink with me! What the hell has that—"

"Did she, Mis-ter Hanlon?"

"Well—I—I believe she did. She was in my suite tonight. She usually stops by at least once a day, and we usually have a drink together."

"Uh-huh. Sounds real homey. Got any chloral hydrate around your suite, Mis-ter Hanlon?"

"I believe so. I had a prescription for some. I seldom use it because of the after-effect, but—"

"Then you got practically all of it left, right?"

Hanlon started to nod. Then, caught himself, remained silent for a moment.

"You don't need me to tell you, do you, Ford?" he asked quietly. "If you knew I had some, as you undoubtedly did, then you know how much I have left. You already had the answer to every question you've asked me. Now, what are you implying? That I doctored my wife's drink with chloral?"

"We-el . . . Don't hardly believe implyin' is the right word."

"I see. You really think I'm stupid enough to do a thing like that?"

"Well"—Ford's eyes glinted. "You was stupid enough to chisel a lot of folks that like you and trusted you. But I guess you wouldn't figure that was stupid, would you? Probably looked on that as real smart."

The old man's shoulders slumped a little. His hands moved in a tired gesture, and then he dropped them into his lap.

"How is she— No, never mind," he said dully. "What's the charge? Murder or attempted murder?"

"Murder."

"I see. The poor damned fool." Hanlon shook his head. "Must've figured on sticking me with an attempt rap, and she took too big a dose. Well. Murder isn't a bailable offense, is it, Ford?"

"Nope. It sure ain't, and that's a fact."

"Then, what are we waiting for?"

. . . At the twelfth floor, Ed Gusick brought the car to a stop, and Bugs—prompted by a nudge from Ford—got off. The deputy also got off and escorted him a few steps down the hallway.

"Want you to stick around your room a while," he said quietly, quickly. "Now, you got that? You understand what I'm sayin'? You ain't maybe in a kind of a daze?"

Bugs nodded. Shook his head. He was pretty well out of the stupor which the rush of events had thrust him into.

"But what—why—"

"Because someone's comin' to see you. And it's damned important that you be there. Wait a minute!"—he peered down the hall. "Ain't that your room with the door open?"

Bugs turned and looked. He heard the faint hum of a vacuum cleaner. "It's just Rosie; the maid, you know. Now—"

"The maid, huh? Well, that party ought to be comin' to see you any minute now."

He clapped Bugs on the shoulder, ran back to the elevator. Its door clanged shut, and Bugs went on to his room.

His head ached. His body was damp with sweat of nervous excitement. He'd *had* it tonight, he thought. If anything else happened before he got a chance to pull himself together—!

He supposed he should feel relieved because Joyce was out of his hair for good, which meant that if Ford ever had been in it, he also was out. He had to be, obviously, since he could only work through Joyce.

So there was much to feel relieved and grateful about. And Bugs was. But not very much. Right at the moment, he couldn't feel much of anything.

He entered his room, nodded an absent greeting to Rosie. Her bright smile faded, and she looked at him anxiously as he dropped into a chair.

"Is there something wrong, Mr. McKenna? Anything I can do for you?"

"Thanks, I'll be all right," Bugs shook his head. "Just a little upset. You see . . ."

He told her about Joyce's death and Hanlon's arrest. Rosie's lovely eyes sickened with horror.

"Oh, how awful! How terrible! You know, Mr. McKenna, she must have already been poisoned at the time I saw her tonight. She didn't look at all well, but she insisted that she'd be all right after she laid down a while. So I just got her suite cleaned as quickly as I could, and left. If I'd only known . . ."

"Forget it," Bugs said. "No way you could have known."

"Perhaps not, but I can't help feeling a little guilty. Are you sure she *is* dead, Mr. McKenna? Not just dying, I mean? There's no chance that they may be able to—"

"No, she's dead. Dead when they found her, I guess."

"How awful!" Rosie repeated. "If I'd only—"

There was a brisk knock, and Amy Standish came through the open door. She was very prim, chilly of manner. As Bugs got clumsily to his feet, took a hesitant step toward her, she gestured curtly to Rosie.

''No, don't leave, Miss Vara. Go right ahead with your work. What I have to say to Mr. McKenna will only take a minute."

"Amy," Bugs said. "I'd like to—"

"Please!" She held up a hand. "I want to get this over with. You're in some kind of difficulty, I believe. I think you mentioned something about it. Well, I don't know whether the amount is sufficient to be of help. But I have five thousand dollars at the house. If you'll stop by I'll give it to you."

"But—" Bugs was starting to scowl. "Where'd you get that much money? Why should you give it to me?"

"Does it matter?"

"You got it from Ford, right? You're trying to help him, not me?"

"Am I?"

"Sure, you are! He can't use me any more. Everything is washed up for good, and if I stuck around I might get to be a nuisance. So this is my payoff. I'm supposed to take it, and get."

Amy smiled peculiarly. A smile of tired and wondering amusement. Bugs's scowl deepened . . . What was so funny, anyway? What he said made sense, didn't it? Well, maybe it was a little odd that Ford would pay him to clear out. Ford could doubtless run him out if he chose to, do it without any fear of repercussions. And Amy could have borrowed the money on her house. But still . . .

He didn't know. He couldn't say why he'd said what he had. It was as though he'd been compelled to. As though some inner compulsion had swerved him out of a smooth path and into a rock-strewn rut.

"I couldn't believe it," Amy said wonderingly. "Lou told me you'd react like this. He told me what you'd say, almost word for word. And I—"

"So he did put you up to it! You admit it."

"Did I? I don't recall that I did."

"But— Well, all right then," Bugs said stubbornly. "Tell me I'm wrong. You tell me I'm wrong, and I'll—"

"I've said all I have to say. The money's at the house. If you want it, I'll give it to you."

"But—"

But she was gone, jerking the door shut behind her. Bugs remained standing, one hand half-extended, feeling very lost and lonely in the echoing silence. *Just ain't happy when things are going good. Can't foul 'em up one way, you'll do it another.*

He heard a faint sound: a suppressed gurgle. Quickly he dropped his hand to his side, and turned, glaring, to Rosie. She was shivering, shuddering with laughter. Her eyes danced with impish merriment.

"Well," he said. "What's so goddamned funny?"

"You," she said. "You are, you sweet, stubborn stupid lummox!"

She came to him suddenly, drawing him into her arms, laying her head against his chest. Her arms tightened, pressing him into the soft length of her body; and then her hands began to roam, probed sensually, delicately.

"Uh, look, Rosie," Bugs began. "I don't think we—"

"No, you don't do you? You don't think at all. And I really think it's pretty wonderful. Do you know, darling, if things were only a little different I'd take you with me. I have more than enough brains for both of us, and you'd be so easy to manage . . . and you are such a pleasant bed companion . . ."

"Rosie!" Bugs said sharply. "I—what the hell is this?"

" . . . Oh, yes, my stupid sweet, I really enjoyed myself

very much. Sex is one thing I simply can't fake about. Of course, sex wasn't my primary purpose. You didn't have the money in your room, so I thought you might be carrying it next to your body. And when I found out you weren't . . . well, you didn't get any more of those letters, did you? And you never saw any connection between the two events, did you? . . . Don't do it, darling! Don't ever try! Because you must have an awful lot of guts—literally, I mean—and these .38 Specials do make such a mess."

She stepped back quickly, levelling the gun—his own gun—at him. She said again, "Don't do it, darling! Don't even look like you're going to. I'd hate terribly to kill you, but—"

"Like you hated to kill Joyce, huh? And Dudley?"

"Who says I did? What proof is there? No, I don't have any murder charges against me yet, and I won't if I can possibly avoid it. So if you'll just take out your car keys and drop them on the floor . . . Come on! Do what I told you to!"

Bugs did it, hastily. Rosalie ordered him to turn around, gesturing impatiently when he hesitated.

"I mean it, darling. I'm trying to be nice to you, but I'm liable to get tired very suddenly."

"But I don't get it," Bugs said stubbornly. "Ford doesn't have anything on you. Why do something that will—"

"But Mr. Ford is a very peculiar man, sweetheart. If he ever got the notion that there *should* be something against me—and I have an idea that he's about to—he'd never stop until he found it. Aside from that, there's nothing more for me to do in this hole. I haven't accomplished what I came here for, but I've made a good start on it. Even after I've deducted for a protracted vacation in Mexico, I'll have practically enough to . . ."

"To what?"

"Sorry. I can't tell you that. Now, if you'll turn around, please . . ."

"Wait a minute!" Bugs said. "You—you're talking about that five thousand? You're going to rob Amy?"

"Of course. But you needn't worry, honey. She won't get hurt at all . . . if she's sensible."

Bugs looked into the placidly beautiful face, a face as free of warmth, as lacking in honest compassion, as something chiseled out of marble. *Sensible!*—he groaned inwardly. What would the word mean to a dame like this? Just how "un-sensible" would you have to be to get the curtain drawn on you?

"Don't do it, Rosie!" he begged. "It's armed robbery; you can get a life sentence for it in Texas. Why run a risk like that for five thousand bucks? You don't have to, for God's sake! Why, a girl with your looks could—"

"Thanks. But believe me, darling, five thousand dollars can be very hard to get. *Particularly* for a girl with my looks . . . when those looks become a little too well known, you know. She finds it difficult to move around where the money is available."

"But, dammit—"

"That's all. Turn around . . . *Turn around or I'll kill you!*"

There was finality in her voice. Bugs turned.

"All right. Now, over to that closet and open the door . . . Tha-at's the way. That's my darling . . . Now get in there!" The gun suddenly prodded him in the back. "Go on, you overgown ox—you can make it! Get in and get down on your knees."

Bugs squeezed and jammed himself into the closet. He went down on his knees.

"Fine," Rosalie Vara said softly. "He's a real nice boy, and now he's going to have a real nice nap."

The gun crashed down on his head. The door closed and the lock clicked.

But Bugs didn't hear it.

It was very peaceful in the large corner room of the city hospital. The lights were dimmed to a friendly glow. The air-conditioner purred sleepily. There was the gently pungent smell of antiseptic, and subdued murmur of voices, intermittent glimpses through the doorway of white-uniformed nurses and white-jacketed men. Life was all around you, all its sights and sounds and smells. Pressing against you, but never obtrusively. Leaving you alone until you were ready to join it.

Mike Hanlon yawned luxuriously, squirmed his tough old body against the cool-feeling sheets of his bed. It was the first time he'd really felt relaxed since he didn't know when. He decided, wryly, that he'd have to get arrested for murder more often; and he said as much to Lou Ford as the deputy came through the door.

Ford sat down, looking a little discomfitted. Hanlon laughed good-naturedly.

"But don't let me take all the fun out of it for you, Ford. I'm okay now, but you really had me sweating for a while."

"Well, now," Ford said sheepishly. "Wouldn't want you to think I did it just to give you a bad time. I had to make it look like a real cinch, or—"

"Sure, you did. I understand, and no hard feelings . . . How's Joyce doing?"

"Still talking ninety to the minute. Nothin' like a person's thinking they're going to die to start 'em to talking." Ford tucked a cigar into his mouth and struck a match to it. "Course she never was in no real danger of dyin'. She got help too quick for that."

"How did that happen, anyway?" Hanlon said interestedly. "You'd anticipated an attack on her?"

"Nope. Probably should have but I didn't," Ford said. "Joyce is alive because she played it smart. She keeled right over and played dead the minute she felt the stuff working on her, so Rosie didn't stick around to make sure that she *was* dead. She beat it, and Joyce was able to use the phone before she passed out."

"I see," Hanlon nodded. "Now, here's something else I don't get. In fact"—he hesitated—"there's damned little of the deal that I do get. I know you're probably tired of talking about it, but if you wouldn't mind filling me in—"

"Wouldn't mind at all," Ford said promptly. "If you hadn't asked me," he added grinning, "I'd probably have told you anyway. It ain't often that I get to take a hand in anything real interesting, and—"

The telephone rang. Ford murmured a word of apology, and picked it up. "Lou Ford speakin' . . . Yeah, well that's good . . . Uh-huh, uh-huh . . . No, I guess I can wait until tomorrow . . . Swell. See you then . . ."

He hung up. Hanlon shot him an inquiring glance. "Was—?"

"Who?" Ford said innocently. "Looky, Hanlon, you did invite me to tell you the whole story, didn't you? You want it all instead of a pecky piece here an' there that won't give me no chance to show how smart I am?"

"Sure," Hanlon laughed. "Not that I need to be shown. Take it right from the beginning, then, with Dudley getting killed."

"But that ain't the beginning. Dudley's gettin' hired was the beginnin'. Why did Westbrook hire him, an' why did he insist that Dudley was on the level, an' why did Dudley turn out to be not on the level?"

"Well . . ." Hanlon frowned. "I'm afraid I don't . . ."

"You'd say Westbrook was one hell of a shrewd guy, wouldn't you? It was his job to size people up, an' he risked that job when he stood up against you an' hired Dudley. Now, why'd he do that, anyway? What made him so sure that Dudley was absolutely okay? Just one answer, isn't there?"

Hanlon hesitated for a moment. Then, he let out a startled grunt. "Why, of course! Westbrook was sure he was okay because he was! He . . . But, Ford, wait a minute. If that was the case, why . . ."

"Why," Ford nodded. "An' that one little why is the key to the whole thing. Dudley was up in his middle years. He'd been in hotel business all his life, and he'd never pulled a dishonest trick before. An' now a good friend had got him into a good job. He didn't have no family dependin' on him. He wasn't in no personal jam where he had to have money. All he had to do was just like he'd always done, an' he was hunkydory. An' he didn't do it. He did somethin' that was bound to cost him his job an' his reputation. He broke faith with Westbrook, an' he knew Westbrook would get him blacklisted in every hotel in the country. In other words, he washed himself up—for a lousy five thousand dollars. Just don't make much sense, does it? Makes a hell of a lot less when you know he could just as easy've knocked down ten thousand. Wouldn't've hurt him a bit more than stealin' the five."

Ford paused to relight his cigar. He puffed on it, grinned enjoyably at the hotel owner. "Well? Gettin' any ideas?"

"None that isn't pretty obvious. All Dudley needed was five thousand. I can't see how he expected to live the rest of his life on . . ." Hanlon's voice trailed away. Then, as Ford continued to grin at him, a slow grin spread over his own face. "Why, hell, yes! That five thousand was supposed to make him rich! He was going to invest it in—well, oil. Couldn't be anything but oil out here. He—but wait a minute! Five thousand is peanuts in a proven oil field. Even if he'd had ten times that much, he couldn't have done anything with it. Well, sure, maybe he could have bought a tiny interest in an operation, but he'd be about as well off puttin' his money in government bonds."

"So we got another of those can't-be-but-is riddles," Ford said. "An' the only person with the answer, as I saw it, was the person that killed Dudley. Which brings us to Bugs McKenna. Now, I ain't got the slightest idea why Bugs did scuffle with him—prob'ly went there as a favor to Westbrook . . ."

"That's right. I'd take an oath on it."

"But Dudley was already a dead man, before he ever tumbled out the window, so we know our killer is someone else. A woman, by all appearances. One of two women. Well, Joyce was out of it, as far as I could see. If she'd wanted five thousand bad enough she could've hocked some jewelry or talked it out of you. So that leaves us with Rosalie Vara. And Rosie's the biggest, dangdest riddle yet.

"A mickey artist is a pro, you know. Bound to have a record somewhere. And Rosie didn't have one. I put out two-three hundred information-wanted's on her—every place big enough for a gal like that to operate—and I didn't turn up a thing. Still I was sure she had to be it, and I got a lot surer when I saw Bugs give her a shakedown as she was comin' out of the Westex City post office. Must've been tryin' to blackmail him, the way I figured—on the Dudley deal, since there wasn't nothing else. She knew he'd been in Dudley's room, so she must've been there herself. Well, she was too smart to let Bugs catch her, but—" Ford laughed gently, absently. "That poor damned Bugs. So scared of doin' something wrong that he couldn't do nothin' right. Should have know I couldn't expect him to cooperate with me, and I guess I've been pretty hard on him. Put him under all kinds of pressure to go bad. But I felt I had to do it, see? There was a third person involved, a young lady I think the world of, and if Bugs couldn't stay straight, no matter what, I wanted to . . . 'Scuse me. Ain't borin' you, am I?"

"No, no, not at all." Hanlon stifled a yawn. "You were saying something about a third party?"

"About covered the subject, I guess. Goin' back to Rosie, and that day in Westex: I had her ride with me on the return to Ragtown, and that hunch of mine just kept growin' and growin'. She was just too good to be true, y'know. Pretty as a picture, nice manners, intelligent, pretty fair education apparently. And so dadblamed honest. Honest in a way that hurt her and didn't do no one any good. I mean, the gal was whiter-lookin' than me. Couldn't be more than a teensy bit Negro, so why make such a big to-do about bein' one? Well, though, I pretended to take her at her face value. Told her I was really after Bugs, and asked her to keep an eye on him for me. And she got all wide-eyed and trembly, but she promised she would.

"Now, o'course, if I'd mugged her or fingerprinted her, I'd've known the truth right away. But I didn't have no grounds for doin' that, an' unless she was wanted somewhere, she'd be long gone fast. Anyways, a murder had been committed in my county, an' I wanted it solved before I turned her over to anyone else. So I put out another information-wanted on her—practically the same one I'd put out before except for one word. I didn't identify her as a Negro.

"Well, hell. You never saw anything like it. Must have got fifty replies on her. Looked like she'd been workin' the chloral hydrate before she was old enough to walk. No, she wasn't wanted for anything right at the moment. All that these different places wanted out of her was to keep the hell away from them. And any time she showed up in one of 'em they gave her the roust.

"They had plenty more to say about her, none of it flatterin', but I'll just hit the high spots. Her folks came from here, and they were pretty good people. Poor but honest.

She was of Mexican or Spanish descent. Her real name was Vera Rodriguez . . . Oh, yeah, and she had a pal named Joyce. And Joyce had disappeared from her usual haunts about two weeks after Rosie did.

"Yeah, it was the same Joyce—your wife. Rosie came here first, an' then Joyce showed up. Looked to me like Rosie must have sent for her.

"Well, I began to get the framework of the story about then. T'see how it just about had to shape up. Rosie was layin' low, but why'd she travel fifteen hundred miles to a town where she couldn't operate and she didn't know no one? She had to have a reason, a mighty good one. And she had to have it before she came here; it couldn't be somethin' she run across afterwards. Only thing I could think of was that it must be somethin' connected with her folks, and since her folks was Spanish or Mex....

"Maybe I better tell you that I'm part Spanish on my mother's side. Some of my ancestors came over here way back in the sixteenth century, and one of 'em got a whopping land grant from the King o' Spain. God knows how many times the title changed hands in the next three-four hundred years, but it *had* existed, an' if a person could prove it, like I could, and if he could prove that he was a descendant of the original grant owner—like I could—he'd be in a pretty nice spot. He'd have a hell of a time takin' the land away from the current owner; probably wouldn't live long enough to fight it through the courts, and it'd cost him more than it was worth if he did. But he could make one awful nuisance of himself. You know, he could cloud the title to the property. Keep it from bein' sold. Stop any business havin' to do with it from being transacted. In the end, if you were the owner of the property, you'd just about have to cut him in with you.

"Yeah, that's where my money comes from. Drawin' a percentage of production from two oil companies over near Westex. I had to swear to keep quiet about it, naturally, because a lot of people around here have at least a little Spanish blood and it might give 'em some ideas. But it'll all be comin' out in court now, anyways, so— Say, you are gettin' tired, ain't you? Maybe I better—"

"Huh? No, I'm fine," Hanlon protested. "Just resting my eyes for a moment."

"Well, I'll wind it up fast. Cut out my surmisin' and deductin', and tell what actually happened ... Spanish people take a lot of pride in their ancestry, and a lot of Mexicans like to claim Spanish descent. So Rosie's dad told some pretty tall tales about what big shots his ancestors had been—stories he'd probably heard from his own folks. And when he died he left her a number of old papers and maps and legal-lookin' documents. Well, the time comes when she's got to lay low for a while, go some place where she ain't known. So she takes this stuff to some lawyers to see if she can cash in on it. They tell her she can; that she's got a bonafide claim to several thousand acres of this country. But they'll need a five-thousand-dollar fee to prove the claim in court.

"Now, that was a dead give-away right there. It proved they were shysters. Because if the case had been that much of a sure thing, they'd've wanted to take it on a percentage basis. But Rosie fell for the story, probably talked herself into it as much as they did. And since she had to do some travelin' anyway, she came here to see just what she had claim to. An' what it was, o'course, was your holdings. Millions and millions of dollars and all she needed to get it was five thousand.

"Well, bein' so close to that kind of dough, she didn't like to take any chances. So she sends for Joyce, promisin' to cut her in on the deal. Joyce has been mixed up in some off-color stuff, but nothin' really serious. In a boom oil town, it won't be no trouble at all for her to gold-dig a few thousand bucks.

"Howsome-ever, Joyce looks the situation over an' she gets a lot better idea. Why split with Rosie—an' she don't exactly trust Rosie, any more than Rosie trusts her—when she can grab the whole hog for herself? So she marries you, and right away she starts figuring out how to get rid of you. She was afraid if she didn't do it pretty pronto, y'see, if she waited to inherit in the normal course of events, you wouldn't have nothin' for her to get. She had to grab the property and cash it in, or Rosie would take it away from you.

"Naturally, she couldn't blow the whistle on Rosie. If she did, Rosie would do some talkin' herself, more or less prove that the marriage had been entered into in bad faith, which would be grounds for havin' it dissolved. So Joyce stalled, tried to kid Rosie that she was doin' her best to squeeze five thousand out of you. An' I guess you know that Rosie wasn't kidded a bit. She pretended to be; she'd visit Joyce in her suite and everything would be friendly as hell. Meanwhile, however, she was working on Dudley. Gettin' him to steal the five thousand for a half-interest in her claim.

"He steals it. She bumps him off, because she never had no intention of splittin' with no one. But somethin's happened to the money—just what I don't know, but I reckon I will some day. Anyway, she thinks Bugs got it, and she tries to get it out of him. Until she's finally convinced that he don't have it.

"Well, according to my calculations she'll look around for another sucker . . . and I plant one on her. A guy that'll grab her when she tries to bump him off. But Rosie's afraid to move just yet, and if she can get Joyce out of the way she can take all the time she wants.

"So, while she's workin' in your suite, she taps your chloral hydrate, like she did, yeah, when she killed Dudley. She fills up the fountain pen or cigarette lighter, or whatever she carries the stuff in. Then, she drops in for a visit with Joyce, and dumps most of it into Joyce's drink. Joyce keels over. Rosie washes their glasses and puts 'em away, then puts the rest of the chloral into an empty perfume bottle. It's supposed to be suicide, see? Joyce supposedly killed Dudley, an' now she's gotten scared or remorseful an'— 'Scuse me."

Ford picked up the phone again. He said, "Lou Ford speak—oh, hello, Amy, how are you? Understand the boys grabbed Rosie without no trouble."

"Never mind about Rosie!" Amy snapped. "Mac just got here, and—"

"Figured it was about time," Ford chuckled. "Bet he ran all the way from town, didn't he?"

"Yes, he did, the poor darling! He was actually crying, he was so afraid something had happened to me. And—you stop that laughing, Lou Ford!"

"Me?" Ford grinned. "What's the matter, Amy? Almost sound like you was mad about somethin'."

"You're doggoned right, I'm mad! You lied to me, Lou! You promised me he'd be safe. You said he couldn't be hurt a bit. Y-you said that she—she'd—" Amy choked with fury, and her voice broke. "S-she—why, it's just terrible! He's got a lump on his head as big as an egg!"

"No kiddin'," Ford said. "Well, I don't imagine it hurt him much. Prob'ly went to sleep right afterwards."

"You just wait, Lou Ford! Just wait'll I get my hands on you! I'll— No, you may not talk to Mac, and I'm not letting him talk to you! I've got him lying down with an ice-bag on his head, and he's not getting up until I say he can."

Ford's face tightened, pain stabbed through his heart, flooded the jeering black eyes. For a moment his world had been penetrated—that private, one-man world—and he knew a sense of loss so great that it was almost overwhelming.

"That's real good, Amy," he said gently. "You keep on takin' care of him that way, don't never stop. Because he's a mighty nice fella, and I know he'll take good care of you."

"Lou!" she said quickly. "Wait a minute! I—"

But Ford had already hung up the phone.

He bit the end from another cigar, tucked it into his mouth. He flicked the head from another match. "Now, about that missing five thousand," he began. "I don't know what—"

A soft snore interrupted him. Hanlon's mouth was slightly open, and his eyes were firmly closed. And he slept the peace of the just. Or the adjusted.

The loneliness swept over Ford again, the loneliness and the bitterness. But only briefly; it was gone almost as soon as it came. He grinned and stood up quietly. He tiptoed out of the room.

He went down the hall, Stetson shoved back on his head, cigar gripped between his teeth, rocking in his high-heeled boots. Laughing at himself, jeering at himself. Laughing away the unbearable.

He reached the entrance, and he stood there for a moment. He breathed in the cold air of darkness and stared up into the heartbreaking beauty of the Far West Texas sky.

It sure was a fine night, he decided. Yes, sir, it sure was, and that was a fact . . .

VINTAGE CRIME / **BLACK LIZARD**

___ **Carny Kill** by Robert Edmond Alter $8.00 0-679-74443-6

___ **Swamp Sister** by Robert Edmond Alter $9.00 0-679-74442-8

___ **The Far Cry** by Fredric Brown $8.00 0-679-73469-4

___ **His Name Was Death** by Fredric Brown $8.00 0-679-73468-6

___ **No Beast So Fierce** by Edward Bunker $10.00 0-679-74155-0

___ **Double Indemnity** by James M. Cain $8.00 0-679-72322-6

___ **The Postman Always Rings Twice** $8.00 0-679-72325-0
    by James M. Cain

___ **The Big Sleep** by Raymond Chandler $9.00 0-394-75828-5

___ **Farewell, My Lovely** $10.00 0-394-75827-7
    by Raymond Chandler

___ **The High Window** $10.00 0-394-75826-9
    by Raymond Chandler

___ **The Lady in the Lake** $10.00 0-394-75825-0
    by Raymond Chandler

___ **The Long Goodbye** $10.00 0-394-75768-8
    by Raymond Chandler

___ **Trouble Is My Business** $9.00 0-394-75764-5
    by Raymond Chandler

___ **I Wake Up Screaming** by Steve Fisher $8.00 0-679-73677-8

___ **Black Friday** by David Goodis $7.95 0-679-73255-1

___ **The Burglar** by David Goodis $8.00 0-679-73472-4

___ **Cassidy's Girl** by David Goodis $8.00 0-679-73851-7

___ **Night Squad** by David Goodis $8.00 0-679-73698-0

___ **Nightfall** by David Goodis $8.00 0-679-73474-0

___ **Shoot the Piano Player** $7.95 0-679-73254-3
    by David Goodis

___ **Street of No Return** by David Goodis $8.00 0-679-73473-2

___ **The Continental OP** $10.00 0-679-72258-0
    by Dashiell Hammett

___ **The Maltese Falcon** $9.00 0-679-72264-5
    by Dashiell Hammett

___ **Red Harvest** by Dashiell Hammett $9.00 0-679-72261-0

___ **The Thin Man** by Dashiell Hammett $9.00 0-679-72263-7

___ **Ripley Under Ground** $10.00 0-679-74230-1
    by Patricia Highsmith

VINTAGE CRIME / **BLACK LIZARD**

___ **The Talented Mr. Ripley** $10.00   0-679-74229-8
     by Patricia Highsmith

___ **A Rage in Harlem** by Chester Himes $8.00   0-679-72040-5

___ **Shattered** by Richard Neely $9.00   0-679-73498-8

___ **The Laughing Policeman** $9.00   0-679-74223-9
     by Maj Sjöwall and Per Wahlöö

___ **The Locked Room** $10.00   0-679-74222-0
     by Maj Sjöwall and Per Wahlöö

___ **After Dark, My Sweet** $7.95   0-679-73247-0
     by Jim Thompson

___ **The Alcoholics** by Jim Thompson $8.00   0-679-73313-2

___ **The Criminal** by Jim Thompson $8.00   0-679-73314-0

___ **Cropper's Cabin** by Jim Thompson $8.00   0-679-73315-9

___ **The Getaway** by Jim Thompson $8.95   0-679-73250-0

___ **The Grifters** by Jim Thompson $8.95   0-679-73248-9

___ **A Hell of a Woman** by Jim Thompson $10.00   0-679-73251-9

___ **The Killer Inside Me** $9.00   0-679-73397-3
     by Jim Thompson

___ **Nothing More Than Murder** $9.00   0-679-73309-4
     by Jim Thompson

___ **Pop. 1280** by Jim Thompson $9.00   0-679-73249-7

___ **Recoil** by Jim Thompson $8.00   0-679-73308-6

___ **Savage Night** by Jim Thompson $8.00   0-679-73310-8

___ **A Swell-Looking Babe** $8.00   0-679-73311-6
     by Jim Thompson

___ **Wild Town** by Jim Thompson $9.00   0-679-73312-4

___ **The Burnt Orange Heresy** $7.95   0-679-73252-7
     by Charles Willeford

___ **Cockfighter** by Charles Willeford $9.00   0-679-73471-6

___ **Pick-Up** by Charles Willeford $7.95   0-679-73253-5

___ **The Hot Spot** by Charles Williams $8.95   0-679-73329-9